When Two Hearts Embrace

Gymaco Brooks

This is a work of fiction. Names, characters, places, and incidents either are the product of the author's imagination or are used fictitiously. Any resemblance to actual persons, living or dead, events, or locales is entirely coincidental.

Published by Donahue Publishing

First Edition

ISBN: 979-8-89864-010-1

Printed in the United States of America

For information about special discounts for bulk purchases, please contact Donahue Publishing at info@donahuepublishing.co.

www.donahuepublishing.co

Dedication

This story is for all of those in the world who have experienced the pain of heartache, heartbreak, and the loss of that special someone. I know your hurt and I know how everything just feels like it is over. Maybe right now it is, but that is only if you let it be. The love of being loved is beautiful. Remember those good feelings, and if you give yourself a little time you will experience that joy of love again...

Acknowledgement

My purpose for writing this work of fiction, at the time that I began to, was truthfully to prove a point. It was pretty much me saying: *I am writing—hey, I'm a damn writer! Now, watch me work my pen...*

A great many people tend to judge others whom they think they know. We all have a hard time giving someone else the benefit of the doubt. *Maybe he can change; or let me show her a better way to do this or that.* In most cases it is due to the way that a person has been living for a certain amount of time.

The time I have wasted is one of my biggest regrets. You know—the time I have spent in one prison after another, remembering all of the dumb things that I was brave enough to admit to! Well, I mean to myself, anyway. I have been in love and I have fell hard. Those tears that come zipping through your being—you know those most painful moments when you catch hell breathing, because the hurting is consuming all of your strength. Each book that I write holds inside of it that sturdy spirit of my life to a degree; but remember, it is a work of fiction. No person at any time is real.

Please know, my friends—the readers—that I love what I do. When I gain your comments, good, bad, or so-so, they motivate me; and I hope that it shows with each new novel. Enjoy this story, because I give you the raw, uncut truth that's a part of relationships. Thank you!

— Gymaco

Roselyn Moore, 31 years old, is a sassy, sophisticated, complicated sister. She enjoys the luxury of fine clothing, classy events, and her own independence. She says no man can fire up her excitement like being single—well, until she meets her match...

Keith Baylor, 32 years old, Mr. Hustle—believes that nothing but the best should go onto his person. If it's not top of the line, the brother will not look at it twice. Keith feels that women are to be enjoyed for a little while and he moves on—well, until he meets his match...

It's true that two people can fall completely in love, in one powerful union. A love so special that when they are apart, these same two people cannot wait to once again be together. Their love is theirs alone and their life is their love, for it is what makes them complete. Can you imagine the emptiness either one of them would feel if their other half has been taken away? Your heart becomes empty, and in love's place lives hurt...

Contents

Chapter 1

Atlanta is filled with energy, and Keith is alive with the sparks that radiate on Saturday nights in the state of Southern hospitality. It is a Saturday night almost like any other, except that on this night, **Keith Baylor** is going out alone.

After taking a good, long, hot shower, the independent hustler takes out a few minutes to pick out something fly to wear to go with his mood. He settles on a money-green gator vest with a cream silk back, a pair of tan **Armani** pants, and a pair of money-green gators—the best for his feet. Dressed to impress as casual, Keith smiles at his image in the full-length mirror on his bedroom door.

"Now, for the icing," the handsome 32-year-old says to himself as he sprays on some **Grey Flannel** cologne. Putting on his **Perry Ellis** eyeglasses, grabbing his car keys, and getting ready to get into traffic, his house phone starts ringing.

"Run your mouth," Keith says into the receiver.

"What's up, player?" **Nique** replies.

The two men were more brothers than best friends, and like all best friends the telephone was vast—an extension in their relationship.

"What's happening?"

"Ain't shit, my man. The same old, same. So what's the move?" Nique asked his partner.

"Oh, shit, dog, I'm about to do a little club-hopping and see what's what around the city."

"Damn, playboy, I wish that I could join you on that more; but dog, I'm beat. My black ass has been working all damn day, son."

"I hear you, Q, and you know that I feel you, real talk. But dig this, cat: I'm about to get in traffic. Let me hit you up tomorrow evening."

"That's a bet. Catch me later, dog. Check it," Nique said before hanging up.

It was 10:30 at night when Keith pulled into the parking lot of the **ESPN Zone**. Keith noticed as he sat inside his ride that the parking lot was packed, so he pressed number 4 on **Donell Jones—"Where You Are."** As the smooth sound from Donell came pumping out of the speakers of his white **Chrysler 300**, Keith found himself being carried away with the music.

Slowly the need came over him—a strong, almost overpowering desire to share his company with a special woman. Keith ran down the list in his head of all of the females that he would occasionally spend a little time with, but not one of them got his blood excited. He was in the mood for the type of woman that can only be classified as a queen, because tonight nothing else would do.

As he sits up thinking about getting cut into the song, it comes to an end. The feeling comes over him that this is not the place he really wants to be, so he mashes repeat on the song, puts the car in drive, and pulls off.

For an hour the independent hustler rides around trying to find that spot—looking for that certain place which would tell, *"Hey player, try me."* As he rolls down **Virginia Avenue**, **Malone's** jumps into his line of vision and the feeling hits him right in his chest.

The place is packed, so Keith makes his way towards the bar while observing the atmosphere.

"Bartender! Hey—say, bartender!" Keith yells over the sounds of loud music mixed with the crowd's conversation.

"Yes, sir, how can I help you?" replied the female bartender.

"Yes, uh—can I please have a Long Island Iced Tea?"

"Sure, handsome. Coming right up," she said to Keith with a smile.

As Keith takes a sip of his drink, he feels like someone is watching him, so he slowly turns away from the bar to look around—and not two feet behind him there stands a beautiful brown-skinned sister. As their eyes lock onto each other, Keith feels as if his ears start ringing, and the only thing that he could say is, "I'll be damned!"

Neither one of them remembered moving, and the memory of this Saturday night to them both would always be like magic.

"Excuse me there, beautiful—do you mind if I ask your name?" Keith said.

"Well, no, handsome, I don't mind you asking; however, I don't recall hearing you tell me yours," **Roselyn** came back in response.

"Oh, damn—it's like that, huh? I'm **Keith Baylor**."

"And I'm **Roselyn Moore**. My friends call me **Rose**."

For a minute Keith was stuck, at a loss for words, just admiring the deliciously tender, sexy, and sassy woman with a face like **Meagan Good** and a body like **Mary J.** Rose was wearing a cream-white **Christian Dior** pantsuit with a light-green silk blouse, setting the whole outfit off with a pair of light-green stiletto heels.

To anyone looking, a person might assume that the two of them were already a couple due to their color resemblance in clothing. The two of them were so caught up in their own that no words came out of their lips. It was like two children who were meeting for the very first time. In the midst of the crowded sports bar/restaurant, neither one of them was aware of the fact that they were still holding hands—hands delivered to one another in introduction.

Keith finally managed to clear the fog from his mind enough to get his mouth to work.

"Damn, my bad, Ms. Rose. Now, that is an original name that you have."

"True, Mr. Baylor—but so is yours," causing both of them to laugh.

Shortly after the introductions were out of the way and Keith got Roselyn a drink, the couple found a place to sit. Through the course of them getting to know each other, they both agreed that this was the first time that either of them had enjoyed a stranger's conversation and company so much.

Keith, for once, made the decision to break one of his own rules by placing some of what he was feeling upfront onto the table; and of course, if his best friend Nique were there, he would have rushed his partner to the nearest hospital screaming that Keith was dying...

"Rose, can I tell you something?"

"Well, Keith, I don't know. I mean, you said that kind of serious, so I'm almost afraid to hear whatever it is that you want to tell me."

"Oh, no, baby—it's not anything ugly, so please don't panic on a brother, now. To be honest with you, Roselyn, there is an issue of feeling that I was experiencing earlier and I would like to address it."

"Okay, Mr. Baylor, now I am a little bit curious. First you call me 'baby,' and then you come back and say my name in such a way that I find myself enjoying the sound of your voice when you say it; so I think that I would very much like to hear what you have to say."

"Damn, Ms. Moore—you're pretty good," Keith said, smiling.

"Well, thank you, Mr. Baylor. You're not too bad, by the way," Rose came back, and they both laughed.

"Roselyn, have you ever had the feeling that you were meant to meet someone before you did?"

"No, Keith, honestly I haven't. But I can tell you something strange, though. Tonight, I was supposed to meet two of my girlfriends here, but things did not work out. I was on my way home, and as I was driving by I felt like I needed to come into **Malone's**."

"Damn, Rose—that's a trip, because I felt the same way."

"Excuse me—what did you say?" Rose said, sitting up further on her stool.

"I said that I felt the same."

"Oh, Keith, I heard you the first time; but isn't that weird?"

"No argument coming from this end," Keith said, holding both of his hands up in surrender.

This was a striking experience, and they became quiet as the two of them thought about the situation—caught off guard by this unexpected connection, both of them sat there playing with their drinks. Keith sat there watching Roselyn take a sip of her apple martini, gathering his thoughts before speaking. Roselyn found herself completely thrown off balance by this attractive, well-dressed brother with a face like **LL Cool J**. This was truly a strange meeting for them both...

Chapter 2

"Rose, I'm just gon' be blunt with you and say this with no cut on it. I would very much like to make love to you tonight; but I don't wish to cause you to feel uncomfortable with a statement of such disrespect. So can I ask you to walk with me outside to my car?"

The request from Keith was asked with such tender respect that Roselyn found it hard to find an excuse not to. She played around with the many reasons why not to exit out of **Malone's** with the smooth-talking Mr. Baylor, until the final thought was, *"What the hell."*

After helping Rose into his car and getting in himself, Keith turned the ignition and the soulful sound of **Donell Jones** came pouring out.

"Oh—that's my song!" Roselyn exclaimed.

"No shit!" replied Keith. "You won't believe this, but I play this song about ten times a day."

"Damn, this is crazy, because I do too," Rose said, laughing like a small child at a play.

Held captivated by the show, both Keith and Roselyn sat quietly listening to Donell Jones' song **"Where You Are."** It was the beginning of a beautiful relationship—the type or kind of joining where the two people involved have so much in common that it would fill a cautious person with fear.

They enjoyed seeing each other constantly for almost a month—doing everything together from going out to a movie, to taking walks through **Piedmont Park**. The issue of sex never came up between the two of them, mainly because Keith did not want to make Roselyn feel rushed; but the truth was, the more that he got to be with her, the greater his desire for Roselyn grew.

If he only knew Roselyn was feeling that same hunger—that very same blood-rushing, mouth-watering desire that he was. Yet she knew that he was giving her the respect and the time that so many women wanted, needed, and deserved. It made her want Keith even more, and it was a constant battle at the end of those special meetings; especially when they would share one of those kisses that were so tender, deep, and passionate that Roselyn would feel her knees go weak.

Little did she know that Keith was catching pure hell from his best friend about the whole sex issue.

"Damn, Keith, man, I just don't get it, doc. What the hell is it that's so special about this **Rose** chick?" Nique asked his brother while sitting on his bed watching Keith get dressed.

"First and foremost, Q—her name is **Roselyn**, or **Rose** if you like. Second, my brother—our relationship happens to not be about sex."

"Bullshit, dog! This is Q you are talking to, here," Nique said, falling over laughing.

Keith couldn't help but start laughing himself. "Okay, Q, I won't lie, bro. My shit feels like concrete every time that I hear Roselyn's damn voice, man! Fuck, Q, just kissing the evil little witch drives me nuts. Last night I almost had a damn wet dream because the sister had invaded my sleep, and for the rest of my damn day I had to walk around like I had motherfucking blue balls."

At hearing that confession from Keith, Nique started laughing again. A few minutes went by with Keith waiting on Nique to stop laughing, catch his breath, and look at Keith—only for him to fall out laughing all over again!

"Okay, okay, dog—I'm done," Nique managed to say while wiping his eyes. "Damn, Keith, you have always been the one reluctant when it came down to long, extended relationships. I mean, damn—when it came to my form of commitment your black-ass was plain unwilling, with an aversion to being coupled up with any chick. I mean, shit, Keith, let's face it, doc—you were a seriously vicious player. So for me to see you spending all of this time with the same female and then you tell me that you haven't hit the ass? That is some truly scary shit, playboy."

"I hear you, Q—but for the first time in my life a classy female has the ultimate player off balance..."

Roselyn decided that she would be the one to make the first move. It was actually the night of their first concert together—a show featuring **Keyshia Cole** and **Ne-Yo**.

Exactly the same evening of Nique and Keith's conversation, at 5:30, Keith came to pick up Roselyn for the 8 o'clock concert. He came dressed in a royal-blue suede **Sean John** outfit with matching royal-blue **Timberland** boots. When he rang the doorbell, Rose answered—and the thought hit him: *Damn, my baby is looking so good.*

While his thoughts kept screaming, *"Shit! Shit! Shit! If God does not give me some more self-control, I am going to eat this sexy motherfucker alive."*

Roselyn had on a pair of **Apple Bottom** jeans with a royal-blue **Prada** halter top, hitting it all off with a pair of wooden **Gucci** sandals.

"Hey there, beautiful—you ready to ride out?"

"What's up, handsome. I'm almost ready—give me a second to get my purse and house keys. I'll be yours," Rose said, walking off.

"Oh God, how I wish," Keith mumbled.

"I heard that, mister!" Rose yelled back, laughing, as she made her way to her bedroom.

Later on that night after the concert, when Keith pulled into Roselyn's driveway and got out of the car to help her out, Rose looked at him in such a way that he thought something may have been wrong.

"Roselyn, is there something wrong?"

"No, Keith, baby—everything is fine," Rose replied as they stood in front of her door.

"Well, if everything is cool, then why are you looking at me like that?"

"Oh... no reason, Keith. I am just wondering what you are going to be doing tomorrow night around nine or ten?"

"Ah—shoot—nothing, Rose. Why, what's up?"

"Something that I have on my mind. So can you come by tomorrow around nine or ten?"

"Yes, sure. I can be here at 9 o'clock tomorrow night."

"Good, baby. See you then, okay?" Rose said, then gave him a kiss before dashing into her house.

On his way home, Keith said to himself, "Dammit—this woman is slowly driving me crazy..."

Chapter 3

When Keith got to Roselyn's house at 9 p.m., the front door was slightly ajar. He gently knocked before pushing the frame completely open. As he stepped inside, the first thing he noticed were the candles burning all around the room. Like lightning, Keith's pulse began to pick up pace with his mounting excitement.

"Hey, Roselyn, do you want me to wait outside or something?" he called.

"Ah—Keith, I'm in my bedroom. You can have a seat, baby. I'll be out in just a minute."

Right at that moment, Anthony Hamilton's hit "Charlene" came pouring out of Rose's entertainment system. Keith quickly turned around in shock because once again he'd been caught off guard.

"Damn, that's my joint," Keith whispered, sitting on the sofa.

"Yes, baby, I know," Roselyn said, standing behind Keith.

Slowly, Keith turned again—this time determined not to be caught off guard. What he saw took his breath away. His imagination had not fully prepared him for the vision now before him. Roselyn stood barely a foot away, wrapped only in a red silk evening top that opened down the front, the silk belt tied into a bow. She also wore a pair of red spaghetti-strap open-toe heels that set off her red toenails on display.

"Shit... I think I'm having sharp pains in my damn chest," Keith said, drinking down the sight with his eyes.

Roselyn laughed as she approached him, totally enjoying that hungry look in his eyes. "Ahhh, Mr. Baylor—it appears you've finally answered one question for women around the world."

"Oh yeah? And what question would that be, Miss Moore—"

Before he could get an answer, Roselyn was breaking him down with a head-spinning kiss—so passionate, hungry, and mind-blowing that it took his breath away. When she finally allowed him to come up for air, all he could do was rest his head against her own and try to collect his thoughts. Slowly, they shared a steady, tender kiss that said everything without words.

Nothing else was said as Keith stood and picked Roselyn up into his arms, carrying her off into her bedroom.

The bedroom belonged to Roselyn and was also filled with scented candles—the air sweet with raspberry. Keith slowly sat Roselyn down on her bed before kicking off his Air Max shoes and climbing up to meet her, embracing her in another deep kiss. Roselyn lct him know her desire for him was burning just as great. The two lovers were locked into an explosive kiss—the kind where people involved find themselves fighting for sweet domination as the tempo builds.

If Keith thought Rose couldn't shock him further, she put a quick stop to that thought. She took his breath away again, placing her bare hand upon his hot flesh. When he felt her fingers roaming under his Nike T-shirt, a lump of air got stuck in his throat.

"Ahhh—shit, Rose," Keith said in a strained voice.

Rose pulled the T-shirt over his head, then lifted the front of her evening top. At the sight of her deliciously soft skin, Keith almost lost his mind, kissing Roselyn's neck gently, making his way down her sugar-brown body. Once he took one of her breasts into his mouth, Rose drew a deep breath and released it in a greedy moan for more.

"Oh, Keith, baby—yes, baby—now the other one," Rose whimpered.

Eventually, Keith worked his way down between the lips of Roselyn's heat. With fingers light as a feather, her gates soon parted.

There is an art to love-making, and it requires both talent and patience. Some men and women don't obtain those skills until they are older, so it is rare when lovers linger and realize the true art of sexual play. Both Keith and Roselyn were players, strong and stubborn—so the stakes were higher with these two. Neither one of them understood that somewhere in their game the rules had changed, because now their feelings had gotten involved.

Keith slowly began to make love to Roselyn with his mouth, tongue, and lips, bringing her to a release so powerful that she cried out.

"Keith, baby—ohhh... shit... shit!" Roselyn cried, arching her back so she could have all of his mouth upon her.

Seeing the pleasure he'd given Roselyn turned Keith on even more, but he refused to rush the moment. He gave her a minute to catch her breath. Soon he rose up from between her legs, and a tender but hungry look passed between them. Rose gently took hold of his manhood, causing Keith to groan. With loving, careful guidance she led him to the doors of her being, where with one smooth motion Keith entered her completely.

For a few minutes neither of them moved—the joining felt so good they almost refused to. Then, slowly, they began their rhythm. This was truly player versus player—love-making at its finest—because the more Keith gave, the more Roselyn wanted. Soon he found himself pushing Rose's legs all the way back so he could take longer, deeper strokes into her sweetness.

A small scream ripped from Roselyn's throat as Keith's rhythm increased.

"Ahh, Keith! Shit, baby—I'm 'bout to... I'm—" Rose cried out.

"Damn, Rose—ahhh!" Keith yelled, filling up with every inch of his being, causing them both to tremble and couple with a pleasure-filled release.

Chapter 4

“Thank you for calling Bank of America’s corporate office—this is Roselyn Moore. How can I help you?”

“Hey, girlfriend. You nasty, but can’t call nobody,” Annette said with a laugh.

“Oh, hey girl—what’s up?”

“What’s up? Girl, stop! So tell me, bitch—how was last night with Mr. Keith? And don’t leave out no details because I have Poochie’s ass on three-way.”

“Oh hell nah, y’all hoes ain’t shit!” All three women started laughing after Roselyn’s statement.

Annette Longs and Stacey “Poochie” Flint were Roselyn’s best friends since they were children. Annette was the outspoken one of the three—the pretty big girl in school who only seemed to look better and better as she got older. The only problem was, she could never lose weight—but what puzzled folks was that Ann drew men like flies. Stacey, who everybody called Poochie, was the really quiet member of their group—she put you in the mind of the radio personality Porsche Foxx: same sexy, laid-back attitude. Poochie’s problem was that she always got involved with the wrong men. Annette was 32, while Rose and Poochie were both 31; so Ann usually ended up both the driver and the lender of the group.

“Now, if I’m not mistaken, aren’t the two of you at work?” Rose said with a giggle.

“Yes, bitch—but somebody wants to hold out on us. So girl, come your ass clean,” Ann came back.

Rose didn’t get a chance to comment because her boss came to her desk with an armful of paperwork.

“Hold that thought, Ann... Yes, Mr. Green?”

"Roselyn, I need you to go over these complaints with me so we can get them out of the way today."

"All right, Mr. Green. I'll be in your office in two minutes."

Rose waited until her boss walked off before speaking to her friends again. "Hey, you two—"

"Yeah, yeah, we heard," Ann cut Rose off. "But don't think your ass is getting away. Meet us at Main Street Bar at six o'clock."

"Okay, okay, girl—bye," Rose laughed and hung up.

***

"Scott, you can use my guest room. Q should be here in another hour."

"Yeah—he told me he had to drop his daughter off or something. But the game, Keith... what's happening first, doc?"

"Shit, Scott—the fuck if I know. Q said something about us hitting the Main Street Bar & Grill, so I'm cool with that."

"Yeah, playboy, hold on with that. Let me get my fresh on, 'cause I know how you get down," Scott said.

Scott—six feet, a shade under tall—was a 29-year-old thug. His main score or hustle was selling drugs, with a robbery on the side. Keith would sometimes invest a few grand in the drug business through his cousin. Like a religion, four days a week Keith would hit Gold's Gym on Candler (Camelot) Creek Parkway and get his workout on, and every so often Scott would join him. Today was one of those days, because Scott needed to bring Keith some money for a previous arrangement. This was just one of the few things that had Keith's hands into being a hustler—but he had to keep his parole officer out of his business.

Keith had already been to prison twice and he was no fan of that party. So at night—from 6 p.m. until 6 a.m.—he was a training officer for **SuperTight Security**.

None of the three men knew that the same place they were about to head for good food and a drink or two was exactly the same location Annette, Roselyn, and Poochie were already on their way to.

At Main Street Bar:

"Y'all two bitches can never get anywhere on time! I started to get the hell on, but my hamburger is too damn good," Roselyn exclaimed.

"Ah, shit, Rose—don't start," Ann said.

"Yeah, girl—you know I don't like when you threaten to act brand-new," Poochie chimed in. "Besides, it's only 6:30, so don't act like you been here all day."

It wasn't long before the three women had food and drinks in front of them. Rose was enjoying time with her girls—it had been more than a month since they'd been out together.

"Okay, Rose—girl, tell us about your man Keith," Ann said, picking up a hot wing.

"You're not gonna let that conversation go, are you?"

"No, hoe—so spit it out," Ann said, laughing.

Roselyn tried to put on a face like she was shy about the direction of the conversation—but Annette and Poochie knew better. Seconds later they were cracking up like schoolgirls.

"Y'all really are nasty—do you know that?" Rose giggled.

"Whatever, girl—but your ass is still holding out," Poochie finally chimed in.

"Okay, okay, you two... you win." Rose leaned in and whispered something that made both friends' eyes pop. "Sex with Keith was the... everything."

"Wow," was all Poochie could say as she fanned herself with napkins.

Annette recovered first. Rose was smiling like an eight-year-old with a missing tooth; Poochie was still fanning and sipping her drink.

"Hell no, bitch—no, hell no—give us the cards, Roselyn! Dammit, come on with the details."

"See, Ann—your freaky ass ain't right," Rose replied.

"Yes, and I love you too—but come on with the come-on."

"Okay, okay... look—one more thing." Rose bit her lip and grinned. "I don't know if either one of y'all ever—well—been taken down with his mouth before... but trust me when I say this, girls: Mr. Baylor should have a solid gold mouth with a platinum, unlimited tongue."

"Shit, girl—stop! Please stop," Poochie said, crossing her legs in her seat.

"Stop my ass, girl—please," Ann laughed. "Now, Rose—you my girl, and you know I ain't a head queen. I love for my man to hit me hard and deep. So keep it real with a sister—how was Keith's dick-down game?"

"Ah, Ann... let me think on that for a second, because I want to answer accurately."

Ann was about to cut loose on Roselyn until she saw the direction Rose was looking. Keith, Scott, and Nique were coming around the bar—and just as Annette followed Rose's line of vision, Keith came walking toward their table.

Chapter 5

"Say, Keith—introduce us to your girls, partner," Scott mumbled out of the corner of his mouth.

"Pick your own poison, cuzz," Keith whispered back.

Once the three men were standing at the table, they were greeted by a group of female smiles the size you see on a cereal box.

"Hey there, beautiful ladies. I'm **Keith Baylor**, owner of **More Hustle Incorporated**. The short gentleman on my right is my partner, **Nique Robinson**. My man here on my left is my cousin, **Scott 'Pain' Barr**. Gentlemen—the sexy one in the middle belongs to me, and her name is Miss **Roselyn Moore**. Please forgive me, fellas, but I do not know these two good-looking sisters by name—which means that you are on your own." He turned to Rose. "Rose, will you kindly walk with me to the bar?" Keith said, holding out his hand.

After Keith and Roselyn walked off, the other four fell into conversation of their own.

"Oh, that **Ménage à Trois** thing kind of turned me on," Rose said to Keith once they were at the bar, away from their friends.

"What? Dammit, Rose—I haven't heard from you all fucking day and you out here playing?" Keith chuckled. "Girl, your ass needs a kiss for a greeting."

"Keith—getting all emotional," she teased. "I was just playing. The reason you haven't heard from me all day is I had a long meeting and a few other obligations. My fault, baby. You're right, though—I threw a brother a little off balance, you feel me?"

"It's alright, Keith—I understand, for real. But all bullshit aside, your whole take-charge attitude kind of turned me on," Rose added, a devilish twinkle in her eyes.

"Sho' nuff—so what would you like to do about it?" Keith replied, pulling Rose into his arms.

"Down, tiger! I see that momma has your complete attention," Rose laughed, feeling Keith's member pressing against her leg. "Now—about us getting rid of our company first."

"Ah—shit, my bad. But baby, they're grown. They can take care of themselves."

"Yes, boy, they can—but that would be disrespectful to me. Believe that we are here together."

"Alright, baby—you win. So tell me, what's your plan?"

"Well... let's set which one of our friends gets paired with who."

"Shit, baby... I got five racks say Q ends up with the pretty one who could go for being your sister."

"Oh, that's Poochie—her real name is Stacey. And as for your bet—I'll take you up on it, because you are so wrong."

Keith ordered drinks for their friends before returning to the table. Five minutes after they were seated, the vibe had settled and laughter was running ear to ear.

Chapter 6

East Point was a city and county inside Atlanta's metro area. Scott was doing his usual.

"What's up, cuzz?"

"Shit, player—listen. Q just hit me up, told me your boy D.J. is letting the O-Z's go for five dollars a pop—"

"Shit, Keith, I'm caught more right now, dawg. My pockets are fucked up."

"Scott, you just paid me two days ago—so how are you fucked up?"

"A nigga has bills and a wife and children—so I'm out here chasing, you feel me."

"I hear you, cuzz. Well, listen, Pain—meet me at the 76 on Jonesboro Road in about two hours. I should have something for you."

"Check that, dog."

When Scott pulled up at the 76 gas station, the traffic was like the expressway. He told his road dog Babyboy to be cool in the car while he went inside to see if his cousin was there or over at the barbershop—and sure enough, Keith was getting a trim by his favorite barber, Silk.

"Yo, cuzz, what's the move?" Scott greeted.

"Yo, what's up, back—everything is everything. Just give me a minute here and we'll walk," Keith replied.

An hour later, Keith, Scott, Nique, and Babyboy were posted up outside, talking shit. Keith had given his cousin some work, and the plan was to split the profit. Everyone was in a good mood until Babyboy saw a dude that owed him some money. Things turned ugly real fast because nobody knew what was about to go down.

A dark-blue Ford Escort pulled up to a gas pump, and out came a light-skinned, heavyset guy named Polo. As he was taking off his gas cap, everything got shitty.

"Hey, motherfucker—pay up or get fucked up," Babyboy yelled—smack!—slapping Polo in the back of the head with a .357.

"Ugh—ahh—ohh—fuck! Hold up, man—I got you, doc," Polo said, looking up from the ground.

"Yeah right, bitch—I bet you do. Now break yourself or get broke off," Babyboy said, giving Polo a hard kick in the stomach.

Under the bright lights, both Nique and Keith were caught completely off guard by the turn of events. Scott, on the other hand, was suddenly behind the wheel of Babyboy's Buick and driving it up alongside his partner.

"Yo, Baby—take that sucker's whip! Knock rubber, champ!" Scott yelled out the driver's window.

Once the two whips had driven off, Keith's cell phone started ringing.

"Yo—this is me, say what's—"

"Let's walk around a minute, then I'll be out of your hair, son," said Rick, Keith's supervisor.

"You the boss. Let's roll."

Keith and his boss were real cool. They had a better-than-average relationship, so Rick as well as the owner pretty much let Keith do his job without breathing down his neck. Sometimes one of them would show up at one of the sites and Keith would walk around with them and shoot the breeze—just like today.

SuperTight Security's job was to protect company property, so they mostly dealt with truck freight companies, construction sites, and some car dealerships. The only problem for the guards was that no one at the company was licensed to carry a firearm—so if anyone had that type of weapon in their possession, that person was on their own. All the guards had was a radio, flashlight, and a cell phone. The good part was that eighty-five percent of the time the guards could secure themselves inside their own cars.

Keith made the rounds with Rick, then made sure the women employees got safely on their way before he got into his gray Camry (his work car). As he rode around the tractor-trailers, making sure everything was cool, his cell phone rang.

"What's on your mind?" he answered.

"Hey, buddy—this is Jack. Are you working?"

"Shit, Jack—there are only two reasons a man like myself would not be working, and neither one of them is taking place at this minute."

"Boy, Keith—you crazy, I tell you. Well, hell—I'll be in about 10:30, no later than eleven, and three hundreds in my pocket."

"Okay, Jack—I'll have you covered by the time you come in for work."

It was 9:00 when the two men were talking on the phone. Keith parked his car between a set of new 18-wheelers, let his driver's seat back, and took a little sip from a cup of coffee. While he was sitting there enjoying a little peace and relaxation, he started thinking about his conversation with Nique from the day before.

What Q didn't know was that Keith had begun to get his hands dirty more and more—and it was driving him nuts because he was also taking some big losses. Keith was just going through too much to maintain. His family and friends thought Keith Baylor was doing real good, because he was always able to help them with their problems. It was all an illusion—the truth was that Keith was fighting tooth and nail to make his appearance a reality. The image wasn't hard to pull off because the brother always put on the best designer gear. It's just sad how easy it is for people to see a lie and accept it for the truth, mostly because people can be selfish and careless about the hell the next person is going through.

"Well—enough of this line of depressive bullshit," Keith said to himself as he dialed Rose up.

"What's up with you, beautiful?"

"Shit, baby—I'm over at Poochie's. Are you at work?"

"Yep—and I'm bored to death," Keith said, laughing.

"Yes, I can imagine. Are you on Frontage Road tonight?"

"Yep—from 6 p.m. till 6 a.m.—and it's only 9:30."

"Keith, baby... is something wrong?"

"I don't know. I guess that would depend on how you look at my situation."

"Look—don't talk to me in riddles, Keith. What's up?"

"Shit, Rose—God looks out for babies and fools. I know I ain't a baby... so I must be a damn fool," Keith exclaimed.

"Listen, baby—Poochie is about to go out to a movie with Q. I'll be out there in about thirty minutes, okay?"

"That's cool. Let me check in on the radio—I'll see you in a few."

***

Nique installed and repaired elevators for a living. Like his best friend Keith, he had been to prison as well. The difference was that Q made about twenty dollars an hour where Keith made $7.50—but you couldn't tell from their dress codes. Tonight the new couple—Q and Poochie—were going to the movies and then find somewhere to eat a late dinner and enjoy a couple drinks.

Q almost called Stacey and canceled—mainly because he was tired from working ten hours, picking up his daughter from pre-K, and then taking care of a few things for his moms. But beautiful women are a weakness to most men—especially a woman who's funny, sexy, sassy, and smart—so the looks only made it harder to say no.

"Okay, now let me get this right," Nique smirked. "You're a mother, you don't have a man, you work five days a week, you live alone, and you're not gay."

"Oh—you forgot one, Q. I don't have HIV or AIDS," Poochie came back with a smile.

"Damn—my fault, girl. Well tell me, Miss Flint—what does a man like myself have to do to get you in bed?"

"Getting me into a bedroom is not hard, Q. My having sex with you calls for some work."

"Damn—and I thought I might have got lucky and caught myself a freak."

"Why—because you are a freak?" Poochie replied, laughing.

"You damn right I'm a freak—but between working, paying bills, seeing my P.O., taking care of my four-year-old daughter, and just living, shit—I hardly have time to watch a good X-rated movie. Nique, believe it or not, I like you a whole lot—and to be honest, having sex with you has been on my mind. And for your information, I'm a freak too—but that's only with whoever my man is. Now here comes the ugly part—"

"Q, cut in—uh, babe, stop playing now. I'm trying to be serious," Poochie said, punching Q in his arm.

"Okay, sexy—my bad, go ahead."

"The truth is, Q, I like you a lot—but I don't want us to rush this thing and then we both end up disappointed."

"I can understand that—so I'll just be the quiet, silent-type for you. And you can just tell me all your dirty little secrets."

"Tell you my business for what—so you can run and tell your boys? Hell naw!"

"I was hoping you would tell me so that when I'm at home tonight with a case of the bubble nuts, I can play with myself."

Laughing like children, Nique and Poochie spent the next two hours getting to know each other better—and the more they talked, the more they found to like.

Chapter 7

The gift of lovemaking has a value beyond measure. Two people can fit so perfectly that words feel too small to describe what happens when two halves come together and create a whole. So many things develop when the heat of real passion takes over. Sometimes lovers lose that burn for each other—usually because they failed to see, understand, and respect the blessing of being in love, or of having someone love you back. Its true value is priceless, and it takes determination from both sides to honor it.

When Roselyn got to Keith's job, she found her man off balance and not quite himself. They were parked in the very back of the trucking company, an area completely isolated. Outside their cars, they leaned together against the passenger door of his Camry. He was frustrated, but holding Rose in his arms always made him feel ten feet tall.

"Keith, baby—you're getting hard."

"I always get hard for you. I know," he said, grinning.

"I do too, boy, but we're outside and somebody is at work," Rose whispered, trying to pull away.

"Oh, so now you're a chicken, Ms. Badass?"

"I'm not afraid of anything. You be careful what you ask for."

"Yeah, Rose. We're grown. Put up or back up."

"Oh, Mr. Baylor... I'm gonna back up, all right."

Nothing could have prepared Keith for what happened next. Roselyn kissed him with so much tongue and control it left him light-headed. When she broke the kiss, he growled like a pit bull, but she was in charge and had a goal: blow her man's mind.

In a blur she spun around, pressed her back to his chest, reached for him, and squeezed. He nearly hopped out of his shoes.

"Fuck, Rose—I almost came in my pants," he snarled through his teeth.

"Calm down, Mr. Big Man. I got this," Rose said, licking her lips as she glanced back over her shoulder.

He felt his hard length freed, but she wasn't giving him one bit of liberty. She set his hands on her hips, slid her panties aside, and guided him. Keith thought he might lose his mind as this "evil" woman took him to the moon. She backed her hips like she was in a 2 Live Crew video, her skirt rolled up just enough to give him a marvelous view.

A brother can only take so much—especially when he's in love with the woman proving a point. When he felt her tighten around him, he exploded.

"Damn it—fuck, Rose!"

Her whole body flushed hot at the sound of him cry out. When his teeth clenched and his grip locked, her body spasmed and she jammed herself down against him.

"Shit," she grunted, coming hard.

They stood there, breathing, recovering—when his radio and cell phone both lit up. And just like that, the real magic of a real woman had done its work: taking her man's troubles away.

Chapter 8

"Keith, I need to talk to you," Rene said as he slid a box of burnt X-rated DVDs into his trunk.

"Rene, I don't have time right now. I got two more stops before work. Hit me later."

The dark-skinned twenty-two-year-old was getting heated—and it was only a matter of time. Rene was one of those little hood chicks always chasing the latest hustler. Keith had tried to keep their dealings like brother and sister, and he was starting to realize doing business with her was a mistake. Sometimes even friendship is more trouble than it's worth.

He put his key in the door when Rene grabbed his arm. It took everything in him not to slap the taste out her mouth.

"Look, Keith. I know you're not gay, and you don't have a 'bad reaction' to pussy. But you seem dead set against giving me any dick for some jacked-up reason. So do me a favor—stop blowing me off like a crack-head and tell me what's up!"

They were in the driveway of her sister's house in Forest Park. Unbeknownst to Keith, both sisters were peeking through the living-room window almost the whole time. He happened to catch Jasmine and Tonya looking, and for whatever reason, that finally pissed him off.

"You stupid punk bitch," he snapped. "I'm not Pain, I'm not Fat Quan, and I'm not Babyboy—so back the fuck off my nuts. A brother can't even be cool with you? It gotta be some other shit? Fine. Since you wanna play—be ready at 6:30 tomorrow morning."

He slid into the driver's seat and turned the key. "And one more thing—if I come by and your ass ain't ready, there are no second chances."

As he pulled off, his cell rang. Roselyn. A sign he'd made the right call—but pride will push a man into sticky places.

***

Annette, Roselyn, and Poochie were sharing a booth at the Rib Shack when Nique came in to grab food. Rose saw him first and kicked Stacey under the table.

"Girl—what the hell?"

"Hush, Poochie. Your boy just came in. Looks like he got off work."

Poochie popped up, catching him mid phone call.

"Yes, ma'am, I'm 'bout to be there in a minute... Okay, Mama. I love you, Mama. Bye."

When she figured out it was his mother, Poochie giggled. Men and their mamas—always a little awkward.

"You know what? That is so sad," Annette muttered, watching them flirt.

"What's sad?" Rose asked. "They look like they're having a good time."

"It's sad 'cause she ain't even gave him none yet," Annette said.

"Ann, how you just gon' say some shit like that?"

"I can say what I want, Rose. I'm grown. I'm just saying—Poochie's ass is in love with that nigga like some TV shit."

"Ann, you're a trip with your shady ass," Rose said, the good vibe slipping. "Some people really do like each other outside of sex."

"Yeah, right. That's like me saying I like being broke."

The energy turned sour. A few minutes later they were bickering. It escalated fast—earrings off, shoes kicked under the table—until Poochie squeezed between her best friends and shut it down. Rose grabbed her things and left with Stacey, fuming.

***

"Mr. Baylor," called Keith's parole officer from the doorway.

"Right here, Mr. Correll."

They handled the paperwork, then sat.

"According to your pay stubs and this compliance form, your pay hasn't changed," Correll said.

"No, sir. Except nights like tonight. I'm working across town—twelve hours at eight-fifty. Still only paid every two weeks."

"Keith, I don't know how you manage on less than a thousand a month. But you're staying out of trouble, so I'm not going to ride you. I'll be by your house sometime this week, and you're down for a urine test next time you report."

"That's fine, Mr. Correll."

"Good. You can go. I got twenty more to see and five in county jail."

Keith nodded and walked out.

Chapter 9

"Damn—your pussy tight," Scott gritted as he forced Annette's knees higher for a better angle.

Annette had called Pain right after the Rib Shack blow-up. He'd just rolled out of bed at 7:30 and wasn't in a romantic mood. Once she picked him up and they got to the motel, second thoughts hit—but she didn't know how to back out. First time together since meeting, and she thought she was ready. The image of Keith—and how he treated Roselyn—kept popping into her head. Then Scott pushed all the way in before she was ready.

"Ohhh—Scott, wait," she cried, pushing at his chest.

"Hold still, Ann. Relax that shit," Pain ordered, trying to work her open with shorter strokes. Her nails dug his back, and it pissed him off. There was no real heat or care—just the kind of sweaty sex most women hate and most men rarely bother repeating. Only someone who understands that lovemaking is an art can overcome the rush to pound their way to paradise.

He eased almost all the way out, then used small, shallow strokes. The pressure of her nails eased. She started to get wetter; her breathing changed. He lifted one leg on his arm. When he felt her getting close, he put the other leg up and slammed deeper. The animal took over. She felt like it went on for hours; it was thirty minutes, and for Scott Baylor it was over—and never to be repeated.

***

"Pain, we need some weed or something," Babyboy said, bored on the block. "It's slow as hell."

"Let's grab a drink. I'll call Keith."

A couple nights had passed since they'd seen Keith, but everybody knew one thing—he kept good green. By midnight, traffic picked up. The brave dealers were out, paper-chasing in their element.

"Cookie, Rene, Shay—I'm 'bout to turn a block. Y'all need anything?" Keith asked three of the girls who handled some of his business.

"Nah, baby, we cool. You be careful messing with your cousin them," Rene said, watching him get in his car. Three days earlier he'd made the mistake of sleeping with her, and the more she learned about his business, the more he regretted it.

The lot was jammed when Rose called.

"Where you at, baby?"

"On the block. Doing my do. What's up?"

"I just wanna see you before I go home. I'll be there in a minute."

"That's cool. Park by my car," he said, then served a couple more customers. Rose sat and watched her man handle his business for an hour, thinking about the situation he was in. When he finally slid into her passenger seat and reclined, she spoke.

"Keith, we need to talk."

"I'm cool with that. What's on your mind?"

"Can we go somewhere else first? I don't like this scene."

"No problem. Give me a minute to tell cuz I'm bouncing."

She waited, then backed out. Another driver tried to angle into a pump. Horns blared. Before anyone could blink, Rose was out of her car.

"Bitch! If you hit my shit, I'll whip your ass out here tonight. I don't know what the hurry is, but you will get drug," she shouted at the woman in the Blazer.

The woman stayed put; Rose marched back, pulled off, and waited at the exit. Keith's boys laughed.

"Yo, your girl Rose on some real gangster shit," Scott said.

"Let me go deal with Miss Fireball before she decides my ass is next," Keith chuckled.

Rose led him to IHOP in Hapeville. They parked side by side. A few minutes of silence, then she told him what was on her mind.

Chapter 10

"Keith, baby... how long you plan on doing what you're doing?"

"Rose, I can't tell you how long I'll be doing anything. Five years from now? I never planned to be on the block in the first place."

"That's my point. You're smart. You don't move sloppy like a lot of these so-called hustlers. I watched you for an hour—you're nothing like your cousin and his partner."

"Let me give you facts about me—the ones I can point out. I'm thirty-two. I'm a two-time convicted felon. I don't have a trade or a degree, and I'm Black with a parole officer. I got more bills than money. So what do I do if I can't hustle? Two months ago everything was smooth. I never had to sell on a corner. Now my Black ass is out here flat-footing like a two-dollar street hoe."

There was a Crown hotel across the lot where they sat talking. Rose listened, watching his face. It was hard to see a man with so much passion for life out here hustling with all his might. Her heart filled with emotion, and she fought to keep the claws of those feelings from digging too deep.

"Boy, I know your cousin and his partner had something to say before I left."

"Yeah," he laughed. "Babyboy said you stay on it. Said you don't play."

Rose's eyes twinkled. She tried not to laugh, but his smile broke her. The sober mood lifted. They played and joked like new lovers—until Keith suddenly turned up the radio.

"Damn, that's my shit," he said as Anthony Hamilton started singing "Charlene."

"Boy, I thought something was wrong when you jumped."

"Shush—listen to this man's song," he said, eyes closed, caught up.

***

"Roselyn, have you heard from Annette?" Ms. Irma asked over the phone.

"No, Ms. Irma. Not in a few days. Why, is something wrong?"

"Well, baby, I don't know for sure. I been calling her at home and on that cell—nobody answering. I just called her job and the supervisor said she called in sick. My baby could've called her momma if she wasn't feeling well."

"I'm sure Ann is all right, but let me call Poochie and see."

"I already talked to Stacey. She said Annette ain't been around since y'all had an argument. Now you girls been best friends too long to let words come between y'all."

"Dammit, Poochie—your big mouth," Rose muttered.

"What's that, baby?"

"Nothing, Ms. Irma. I'm going by Ann's to see what's going on, okay?"

"Thank you, baby. Y'all like sisters. Okay then."

Rose hung up. She planned to wait till after work, but ten minutes later the feeling that something was wrong wouldn't leave. "Damn it, Ann," she whispered, grabbing her purse and keys.

Driving from Union City to Decatur isn't five minutes. She had time to think about that stupid argument five days ago—something that never should've happened, not worth losing a friend over. She decided she'd be the bigger woman and make peace.

Pulling into Ann's driveway on Fayetteville Road, she saw the navy Altima. No need to knock—Ann opened the door, hair wild, robe cinched.

"Shit, girl—what happened to you?" was all Rose could manage.

"Fuck you, bitch. Come in or stay outside," Ann snapped, turning away toward her bedroom.

"Look, Ann—I ain't gonna be too many bitches. Your mom called me 'cause you not answering your phones. And Poochie done told Ms. Irma we argued—"

"Ahhh," Ann groaned, grabbing her stomach and curling on the bed.

Rose rushed over, fear and alarm spiking. She realized she hadn't been paying close attention. Without thinking, she climbed onto the bed, cradled Ann's head in her lap. Ann started to cry. Minutes passed with neither saying anything. Rose stroked her hair, silent comfort, when Poochie came in.

"Poochie, run a hot bath for Ann. Fix us something strong to drink. If ain't nothing in there, grab cash from my purse and run to the package store, okay?"

Poochie didn't ask questions; their years of friendship didn't require them.

Once Ann was soaking and breathing easier, Rose searched the kitchen for food. Nothing but snack junk.

"Damn. As much as I hate to—let me call Keith and see if he can bring us something," she mumbled, closing the fridge.

Chapter 11

When Annette came into her kitchen, Poochie was handing her a drink, and Rose was on her cell with Keith. Annette just took a seat at the dining table with her glass. Rose noticed how Ann paused when she said Keith's name, but she kept talking like she didn't see it.

"Keith, baby—just pick up some KFC for us and that'll be fine."

"Okay, Rose, but I still need directions."

"Just come down I-20 and get off on Gresham Road. Make a left, then turn right at the third light."

"Okay, okay, I got it from there. I'll call you when I get off the expressway."

Poochie passed Rose a drink when she hung up, and all three of them sat at the table. Rose could only stand the quiet so long before getting sick of watching Ann play with her glass.

"All right, Ann—enough is enough. What the hell is going on with you?"

"Rose, girl, I'm fine, so let it go, okay?"

"Let it go? I only asked you a damn question."

"Yeah, Ann—why you so defensive about a simple question?" Poochie cut in.

"Because my stupid ass made a dumb-ass decision—that's why!" Ann screamed, and started crying all over again.

The outburst caught both women off guard. They shared a confused look—they didn't have a clue what was going on with their friend. The answer came before either could ask again.

"You know the other day, when I was trippin' on y'all? I let my anger get me in trouble. After you two left, I called Keith's cousin Scott and we went to a hotel."

"Ohhh... Annette, please tell me you didn't have sex with Scott," Poochie cried.

"Yes, Poochie—her dumb ass had sex with Mr. Scott 'Pain' Baylor," Rose said flatly. "That's why your ass sitting here holding your damn stomach."

"Look, you two—I thought I could handle the situation. I wasn't looking to get hurt, okay? It was... it was just—dammit, you don't understand." Ann started crying again.

At first Rose was angry—not because Ann had sex, but because she didn't think before acting. They all knew Ann was a flirt eighty-five percent of the time, if not more. The problem was she still hadn't learned where to draw the line, tell the truth, or just back off. Rose made a decision, looking at her friend—not to beat her up, but to talk with understanding.

"Ann, Scott is a thug—not a gentleman—and I'm sure you know that now. If you get involved with men like him, you gotta throw the relationship rule book out the window, because street dudes nine times out of ten don't think like brothers who go to a job every day."

"But, Rose—Keith is a street dude. A thug, as you put it."

"Yes, Ann—he is. But my dude is that one out of ten, girl. Keith is not gonna fuck my coochie like an animal, because he's not an animal. I can look in that brother's eyes and see how much he loves me without hearing him say a word. And you know what, girl—I'm falling in love with him, and it's mostly because he's got a heart of gold and nothing about the way he is is fake."

Just then her cell rang—Keith, getting off the expressway. It wasn't long before he pulled into Annette's driveway. Rose came out to grab the food. After a brief hug and kiss, she walked around to the passenger side and got in.

"Thank you, baby," were the first words out of Rose's mouth—before Keith's lips glued over hers.

"Damn, boy—I've missed you too," she said when her head stopped spinning.

"Yeah, well...I'm not really in the mindset for words," Keith replied, eating Roselyn alive with a steady stare.

The look he was giving was a little unnerving—almost like a very hungry wolf looking down on a sheep. Rose could just about see, touch, and taste the desire Keith was trying his best to control. Those same feelings were passing onto her, and as she felt herself getting wet from the heat of him looking at her with so much need—

Poochie stepped out on the porch. The appearance of her girlfriend was enough to break the spell—for this round at least. The game between these two was far from over.

"Keith, I'm gonna need to talk to you later," Rose said as she rolled down the car window. "Poochie, come help me with this food!"

"Something wrong, Rose? You said it like we have a problem."

"No, there's nothing wrong with us—but I do think I should discuss a situation with you."

They made small talk five more minutes before Keith had to leave. Sometimes even the greatest hunger, passion, desire, and lust have to be put on hold—for something just as important: friendship.

Chapter 12

"Nique, how long have you and Keith been best friends?" Stacey asked, lying in his arms.

"Oh, I guess ten or eleven years now. Why? What made you ask me that?"

"I don't know, really. I just think the two of you are so much alike."

"How you come up with that one, Stacey?"

"Keith the fly dresser—Mr. Always-On-The-Move, twenty-four-seven. You? You work eight to twelve hours, sometimes six days a week—and most of the time it's ball caps and Polo shirts, not suits and ties."

"Yeah, fate happened to catch that part, Q," Stacey teased.

"But besides dressing, both of you act alike—caring and loyal to the people you deal with. Neither of you do needless lies, nor do you beat up on women."

"Stacey, why you hitting me with the Keith comparisons, though?"

"Because I just can't figure out how a person like Scott fits into the picture."

"Stacey—Pain is Keith's cousin. Believe it or not, I've tried talking to my boy about that—but he's stubborn. You gotta understand Keith to really know him. He's a die-hard realist who dreams big, and he's willing to bust his ass to get it. To me, that's one of his short comings too—because none of the people around him look at life like he does, nor do they appreciate the person that he is."

"Q—you give me the impression there are things going on you don't like or agree with."

"That's any friendship. Keith is Keith—no lies, no bullshit, no games. But those shit-eaters he's trying to look out for? They ain't half the hustler, person, or human being that my partner is."

Poochie lay in Nique's arms thinking about how he spoke on Keith. They were comfortable together after having sex for the first time, and as they sat quietly in bed Stacey wondered if she should tell Q about Ann and Scott. Some things might be better left alone, she decided, watching one of the candles burn. A few candles glowed around Keith's guest den room earlier—it was relaxing—and there was no sense spoiling a good day.

***

"Say, Keith—let me get two dubs of green," yelled Cap, the tear-through-shoes pimp, strolling up to Keith's car.

Pain and Babyboy fell out laughing when they saw the would-be pimp—neither man had any respect for the brother. Pain considered Cap more trick than pimp, while Babyboy thought he was a joke. Keith felt different: every man is entitled to put his hustle down however he's able, so he never gave Cap a hard time.

They shared a little small talk. Keith handed over two twenty-dollar bags of weed at the car window.

"Cap, my man—you given up on the blow game, huh?"

"Yeah, yeah, Keith, my man. These hoes got me coming and going with this pimpin', so I really don't have time for nothing else, you feel me?"

"I hear you, Cap. Keep it pimpin', playboy," Keith said.

"You damn right, Keith—'cause I'ma check these hoes rain, sleet, or snow, you feel me? Hook, I'm gon' catch up with you later. You make sure my bitches on the playground stay clean, you feel me," Cap grinned, dap'd Keith, and walked off.

As he walked away, the three of them cracked up, making Cap look back—which only made them laugh harder.

It was a pretty average day on the block. Customers of every color came looking for their particular poison.

That's where Roselyn found Keith thirty minutes later when she pulled into the 76 for gas. A slick move by Rose—she was trying to see if there was a different side of him than the one she knew.

Keith was at the pay phone making a transaction with a white guy while Rose pumped gas. She was too far to hear what was said, but she could tell by her man's body language he was pissed about something.

The next thing she knew, Keith punched the man in the face. Rose watched Keith start kicking and stomping him as he fell between the phone booth and a small trash can. For maybe five minutes, nobody said a word—people walked by like nothing was happening.

Rose was almost of a mind to run and get her man, but before she could move, Pain was already pulling his cousin away and dragging Keith to Roselyn's car.

"Here, Rose—take this crazy nigga somewhere before jail ends up his next location!" Pain yelled, shoving Keith into her passenger seat.

"Man, cuz—fuck that cracker! This ain't a game!" Keith roared, trying to climb back out.

"Yeah, cuz, I know—but your ass is on paper, and that ain't no game either. Rose—you got this fool?"

"Yes, Scott—I have him," Roselyn replied, still a little shaken.

"Good, babygirl—then ride out, beautiful. I'll take care of his car."

No need for Pain to say it twice. In the streets you learn to protect your own—or watch them fall. Plans and some loyalty—Pain was down with Keith and made sure Rose got him the hell off that scene. Babyboy understood all of it too. First to prey is first to pay—that's the way it is in this world.

Chapter 13

"Have you completely lost your mind, Keith?" Rose hissed as she hit traffic lights. "That was some dumb-ass shit you pulled back there—and if Scott hadn't stopped you, you would've stomped that poor man into the earth. Is this what you do when I'm not around? Like some type of animal?"

Keith took his time answering. He didn't say a word until the very end—and his response was pure thunder, letting Roselyn know she'd struck a nerve.

"Hold the fuck up. Have you all of a sudden grown another head, Rose? Shut up with that twisted shit. Because a nigga's fucked up over you—my business is my business. Your business is your smile, not mine."

"Keith!" Rose roared right back. "How on God's planet you gon' come at me with a statement like that? You're 'fucked up' over me? Correct me if I'm wrong, Mr. Baylor, but that's not the way to tell someone something good."

"Bullshit, Rose—it is what it is! That's y'all like a female—a brother gotta write out a map? Print his feelings off in bold, goddamn blinking letters on street signs? Does it even pass your mind that some brothers are better with their actions speaking than their lips? Don't answer—I already know the answer. Hell no, you don't! I'm a street dude, Rose—fighting with all I know how to use to make it. People like that cracker gotta be punished when they fuck up—because their fuckups cost me money. Money, Roselyn, that I cannot afford to lose."

"Keith—money can be replaced, baby. Your life can't. Don't you get it? Nothing—not one single thing in these streets—should hold more value than your life."

"Look... Rose—this conversation—never mind," Keith said, yanking the handle and getting out of the car.

Nique's Lexus was still in Keith's driveway when they pulled up, but Keith wasn't in the mood to be nice to anybody. Telling a woman you're in love with her and not hearing anything close to love back can unbalance the best of men. What Keith didn't know was that Roselyn was smiling from ear to ear as she followed him into the house.

"Roselyn, we can argue all night about what happened—but you need to remember, shit gets real in the streets," Keith said, dropping ice into a glass and fixing a drink.

They were in Keith's kitchen, continuing the argument. Rose was just about to respond, taking a seat at the counter, when he slid her a glass of gin and orange juice and started fixing his own. Just then Nique and Poochie walked in—Q in gym shorts, Poochie fully dressed. Rose was too angry to greet them; she came straight with her reply.

"You act like I don't have any idea what takes place in the streets, Keith. I'm not a damn baby—what's wrong with you?"

"Look—why are we still having this conversation, Rose? Damn it. Let me call Pain and find where he's at with my car."

"Oh, I can tell you where his ass shouldn't be."

"What the hell that supposed to mean, Rose?" Keith stopped mid-dial.

Nique looked confused. Poochie, on the other hand, wore shock. Keith glanced at all their faces and closed his flip phone. Q knew how protective his best friend was about his family and wanted to put a lid on this before it turned ugly—even though he didn't know what was going on.

"Hey, Keith, man, I don't think—"

"Wait one second, Q. I want to know what Rose was implying with that bullshit statement," Keith said, voice cold.

"Keith, baby—your cousin is a dog. That's what I'm saying," Rose shot back.

"Okay—like you telling me something I don't know. Yes, I'm sure you figured that out. But do you know what he did to Ann?"

"No, Rose—I don't. But I'm sure you're gonna tell me."

A deep silence took the room. Rose knew she'd made a mistake coming at Keith like that, but her anger had her talking without thinking. Poochie, always observing, understood this was a battle her friend would have to fight on her own—Keith wasn't her man.

Taking a slow breath, looking into Keith's face, Rose spoke carefully. "Baby... a few days ago, Annette and Scott went to a hotel and had sex. He hurt her, Keith. And Ann's been in the bed since."

"Hold up, Rose—if you trying to tell me my cousin raped Ann, that's bullshit and you know it."

"No, Keith—he didn't rape her or anything, but—"

"But what, Rose?"

"Keith, Annette is very sensitive despite the impression she gives—"

"Okay, okay—now I think I get it. Let me paint this picture, and you tell me if I'm right. Pain and Annette went to a room and had sex. He wasn't gentle or romantic. To top it off, Annette wasn't expecting what she got out the deal. Now the three of you walking around pissed off about it. Hey—correct me if I'm wrong, but isn't that their business, not ours?"

"But, baby—don't you see—"

"Yes, Rose—I see what you're trying to do," Keith cut her off. "You hoping I'll tell Pain to apologize to Annette and check him about being so aggressive. No. That's not my business."

"But, baby—you wouldn't have treated a woman like that," Rose came back.

"Because you went somewhere you shouldn't have, Roselyn. With me, understanding is everything. My cousin, on the other hand, is a take-it-or-leave-it type motherfucker. Which means to me your buddy was expecting Scott Baylor to be something or someone other than who he is."

The whole time Keith was talking, no one else said a word. The silence was unnerving, and the looks he was getting from Roselyn and Poochie were enough to make him reconsider. He drained his glass, glanced at Nique—who threw his hands up in surrender—and finally gave in, picking up his phone.

"Pain. Pain—and more Pain."

"Run your mouth, cuz."

"Hey, playboy—where you at?"

"Shit, cuz—I'm in old Hapeville at Wendy's."

"Look—meet me at the Blazin' Saddle in twenty minutes."

"That's a bet, cuz. One," Pain replied, hanging up.

"Q, I need you to take me to get my car. Roselyn, I'll talk to you later. Poochie—be good, babygirl. I'm going to take a shower," Keith said, leaving the kitchen.

Chapter 14

When Keith got out of the shower, he put on a black Dickies outfit with the matching hat and a pair of all-white Air Force Ones. Nique was in the living room channel-surfing when his partner came out of the bedroom.

They rode in comfortable silence for a while before Q finally asked what sparked the whole disagreement between Keith and Rose.

"Look, dog—it's none of my business, but what started you two arguing in the first place?"

"Q, me and you go way back, man, so I can keep it gutter with you, you feel me."

"No doubt, Keith. You know that."

"Well, dog, I dig the fuck outta Rose—you know what I mean. But the sister always up in a player's business. Tonight I had to put hands on that clown-ass peckerwood Mitch. I fronted this fool five hundred dollars' worth of DVDs and he came to me with some bullshit. Anyway, Rose was parked on the set when I got on that mother-sucker's ass—and you know the rest."

Nique didn't say a word while Keith talked. Sometimes a friend has to say the thing that tastes like bad medicine coming out his own mouth. This was one of those times.

"Keith... you think maybe it's time to give up the game? I mean, for once, man—look at all the shit that's going wrong, dog."

"Shit, Q—and do what? Hell, my man, it ain't like I got a skill or a lot of options."

"Well... how about going back to school? Get a trade or something. You could find something in trade school you'd like."

"Look, Q, I appreciate the advice, playboy—for real. But the truth is I actually thought about all that shit you stressing. So I sat down and added up my math, bills and all, you want—never mind. Let me just give you one run-down. My house rent is $850. My car note is $450. Lights, gas, and water come to about $325. My car insurance is $310. And my cell-phone bill is $90. Now, Q, I ain't even added cable, my parole officer, and shit to eat, but my bills already at nineteen hundred plus. So you tell me how to stop hustling when my bills kicking my ass already."

Nique knew his best friend was telling the truth. Even with his own paycheck, Q's bills were no joke, so he couldn't give Keith an answer. It was frustrating, because Keith was one of those brothers who could do well if he was given an opportunity. Sometimes one brother gets a break, another doesn't—and it hurts more when that next brother is your partner and best friend.

Babyboy and Pain were already standing in the Blazing Saddle parking lot when Q pulled in, so there wasn't any waiting around for his cousin to show up.

"Slide, Q—I'll catch up with you later, doc," Keith said as he hopped out.

"That's a bet, playboy. Be careful. One," Nique replied.

The Blazing Saddle had a mix of dancers—Black, white, tall, short. Most hustlers who came in just enjoyed the no-stress vibe the dancers created. Keith picked a table. Babyboy went to the bank window, and Pain stopped to talk to a stripper who went by "Hot Chocolate," one of his on-the-side chicks.

A few minutes later "SoBlack" came over to Keith's table, gave him a quick kiss on the cheek, and sat down. It was a real surprise to the six-foot, caramel-skinned Tameka Perry, because she hadn't seen the Baylor crew in over a month. She considered Keith a little more than an occasional sex partner—they were super cool friends—but there was an unspoken opening that, if either one was interested, their relationship could go deeper.

A waitress dropped a pitcher of beer and filled Keith a glass. He tipped her ten and lit a Newport.

"Black girl, you know I don't really do the strip-club scene," Keith said, blowing smoke.

"I'm aware of that, Keith—but it's good to see you anyway," Tameka replied, looking at him with real care.

"Yeah, well, I'm glad to see you too. But look—I need your help, Tam."

"Oh, now we come to the heart of the matter. What is it this time, Keith—a little weed, some powder, or crack? Oh, my bad—maybe you need help selling some of those nasty movies, huh?"

The edge in her voice made Keith look at her hard. She already knew how sensitive Keith Baylor was when it came to his pride; this was how she chose to punish him for neglecting their friendship. The reaction she got wasn't what she expected.

"You know what the difference is between accomplishments and bullshit, Tam? Accomplishments can mean anything to you—something simple like paying your car note, making somebody you care about smile, even owning your own business. But to somebody else, it can all add up to the same value as crap—spit, trash—just plain bullshit. Those little accomplishments don't mean one wide thing to the world; they only matter to the individual."

Tameka was shaken and off balance—not just by the words, but the truth in them—and by how cold and quiet he delivered his pain.

"You still haven't told a sister what you need, motherfucker," Tameka said, smiling.

"Can you spot about three stacks? I can give it back in about two weeks," Keith answered, trying not to laugh.

Chapter 15

Their conversation didn't last but a few more minutes before Pain came over and took a seat.

"What's up, big girl?" Pain said, pouring himself a glass of beer.

"Nothing much, Scott. Long time no see."

"Yeah, I know—but a player been busy."

"I can understand that," Tameka replied, standing. "Keith—come back at four a.m., okay?"

"Okay, babygirl. I'll be here."

Both men watched SoBlack walk off and instantly find a customer. Around the club, girls were either dancing, talking to other dancers, or trying to entice potential clients. It was after midnight on a Tuesday rolling into Wednesday; business was starting to pick up.

Keith was replaying his conversation with Roselyn earlier, so he didn't hear his cousin at first.

"Starship to Keith. Starship to Keith Baylor," Pain repeated.

"Oh—shit. What you say, cuz?"

"I said, don't you miss tappin' that pretty Black ass?"

"Yeah, cuz—yeah. But me and Tam just cool, dog. Cool is all."

"Dude—that's one sister who would have your children and more to the damn moon with your crazy ass, if you asked her to."

"Nah, cuz—it ain't that kind of party. But check it, Scottie—what's up with you and Annette?"

"Where the fuck that come from, nigga!"

"It came out my mouth, player. What—the fuck, you can talk to me about Tameka but I can't ask you about Annette?"

Pain gave his cousin a hard, searching look before he answered. Something didn't feel right about the question.

"Yo, cuz—you can ask me about the queen of Spain far as I'm concerned. That bitch ain't my woman, so she just another piece of ass. You feel me?"

"No. Hell nah—I don't feel you, because you getting all defensive on a brother. What the fuck's up!"

"What's up, Keith, is there ain't one chick in here even looks like Annette. Second, cuz—you ain't the type of motherfucker who gets all up in another brother's business."

Keith could tell his cousin was losing his temper, so he shifted approach. This is why you don't jump into relationship business with friends or family—no way to tell how the other person will take your intrusion, no matter how careful you are.

"Scott—Rose told me about what went down with you and Annette."

"Oh—so now you wearing capes for bitches, cuz?"

"Damn it, Scott—I'm talking to you as your cousin. What the fuck is this 'save-a-bitch' shit?" Keith snapped, anger flashing in his voice.

People at nearby tables turned their heads, thinking it was about to get ugly between the two men. There was nothing to look at—Pain started laughing so hard tears came out his eyes. Soon Keith just shook his head, lit another cigarette, and laughed with his cousin. When the laughter died, Keith finished the point.

"Okay, cuz—don't bite my head off, dog. Hear me out, and the rest is on you. Roselyn told me Annette is one of those sensitive females who hides her feelings under other shit. Now, I know you might not give a fuck about her feelings—but my advice is, at least take a few minutes for the sister. I mean, hell—you don't know when you'll need her, you feel me?"

"Look, Keith—cuz—I'm not you. I don't open doors for bitches and shit like that. But I don't knock you, 'cause that's your thing.

However… I'll take your advice—mainly because I love you, and also because you just told me some good shit."

***

SoBlack had a condo in Roswell that could take a rich man's breath away. It took her a little over three years to get the place furnished exactly how she wanted it, and Tameka Perry spent every single dollar wisely: a king-size oak bed with antique oak dressers—and somehow she'd even managed to obtain a full-length mirror made in 1872.

Keith had a serious appreciation for this sister's crib, thanks to his love for expensive things. He was one of the few men ever allowed inside; that was one rule Tameka didn't plan on changing. As always, a brother will make himself at home in anyone's house—and when Tameka came out of her bedroom wearing a robe, she found Keith in her kitchen drinking a glass of grapefruit juice.

"Ahh, Mr. Baylor—here's the money you asked for," Tameka said, one hand on her hip, the stacks of bills in the other. "I'm gonna take a shower and go to bed—just lock the door on your way out."

To describe what unfolded between them might take a minute, because nothing can be left out. Watching a panther move on a nature program is the closest comparison to Keith's smooth, controlled way of handling Miss Tameka Perry.

No warning—he gently set the empty glass in the sink and turned toward her. "So you just gonna throw a brother out at one in the morning, huh?"

Tameka's mouth went dry at the hungry look in his eyes. A shiver of excited fear ran through her body. She stood perfectly still, watching him approach with so much controlled confidence. A faint smile touched his mouth as he stopped in front of the taller, dark, arresting woman. The powerful pull she felt toward Keith Baylor was quickly getting out of control, yet she couldn't move or take her eyes off him.

"You beautiful Black bitch," he murmured, voice low. "You know damn well it's going down—so stop bullshitting with me and let's play. Now kiss me, Tam—kiss a real nigga and don't hold shit back."

As soon as Tameka locked her lips to Keith's, the money slipped from her hand and scattered across the kitchen floor. Their tongues did the ghetto tango, heat turning electric. Keith scooped SoBlack up into his arms and carried her to the bedroom. The twenty-seven-year-old sister was so dazed she could only go along with what was happening.

As Keith untied her robe, his cell started ringing.

"Keith, baby—that might be an important call," Tameka managed, her voice trembling.

Instead of answering, Keith took in the full view of her body with the eyes of a hungry hawk that's trapped a mouse. No false expectations. No lies. No games. Not a single word, as he set the phone on the floor beside the bed, stripped, and climbed over her.

He was filled with a primitive possessiveness he would later ponder in deep thought. This wasn't the first time they'd been sexual, but it was the first time either had experienced this kind of power between them.

"Keith, baby... please wait—I need to—ahhh!"

That was as far as she got before he slid fully into her softness. She trembled with delight as ripples of pleasure shot through her whole body. He gave her only a moment to adjust before he pulled almost completely out and drove back in deep. Again and again—Keith eased out of that sweetness, slowly increasing their tempo. Sweat ran off their bodies until a brutal tremble of ecstasy hit Tameka, making her whimper and fasten her mouth to his. That was more than enough to drive him crazy—control disappeared. With a mighty thrust, Keith drove hard and deep into her hot, moist center and exploded.

They lay together, spent, unable to move. The last sound either of them heard was Keith's cell phone ringing again.

Chapter 16

"Poochie, give me a minute, girl—dammit!" Annette yelled from her bathroom.

"Ann, you are so slow. Rose will be pulling up in a few minutes, girl, so hurry up."

The three women were about to go see a movie together. What Stacey and Annette didn't know was that Roselyn was not in a good mood. She'd tried to call Keith that morning before work and there was no answer, and she hadn't heard from him all day. It just so happened she'd been calling at the same time he was in bed with Tameka.

There's a concrete truth to the belief that when your other half is either up to no good or in a bad situation, the other part of your soul will try to connect. Is it something inside us sending off warning signs, trying to convey an urgent message? We may never be able to explain it; I call it one of God's blessings.

Annette was coming out of the bathroom when they heard the horn blowing from Rose's black 2003 Cadillac CTS. Roselyn didn't waste time with small talk—soon as her girls were in the car she was backing out of Annette's driveway and hitting Keith's number on speed dial at the same time.

"Yo—run your mouth," he said, answering on the second ring.

"Oh, so now you decide to answer your damn phone?"

"Damn—and hello to you too, Roselyn."

"Fuck that, Keith. Where the hell have you been that you couldn't return my calls?"

"Oh, damn, Rose—my fault. Baby, I should've told you I'd be out all night selling dick, 'cause my pockets are all fucked up."

"Keith Baylor, that shit wasn't funny, boy. Don't play like that."

Rose had no idea her man was absolutely serious about how heavy his mind was when he got home. He didn't call a soul, didn't turn on the TV, didn't open a newspaper. He came home, took a long shower, put on sweatpants, and sat down to think with a head full of heavy thoughts. When the human heart, mind, and spirit aren't in agreement, confusion takes hold and answers don't come easy. That phase alone can be enough to break a person of weak heart, mind, and spirit.

For a minute Roselyn thought he had hung up, because he went silent.

"Keith, are you working today?"

"Yes. I'm at work now, Rose."

"Okay. I want to see you when we come from the movies."

"That's cool with me, Rose—you know that. I'm in Forest Park tonight."

"Okay, baby. Bye," Roselyn said before hanging up.

***

"Annette, baby—what's up, tits?" Scott said when she answered her cell.

"Uh... hey, Pain. Nothing," Ann replied—both confused and nervous at the sudden call.

"You busy with company or something?"

"Oh—no. Nothing like that, Pain. I just got out the shower, so I was getting ready for bed."

"I can understand that. But check it—can I come by and see you tonight?"

"Scott, I don't know about that. I have to go to work in the morning, so I wasn't planning on coming back out."

"Look, Annette—I've got a set of wheels, so you don't have to move that pretty ass of yours one inch, for real. All I need is some directions on how to get at you."

"Ah, Pain... maybe that's not a good idea. I mean, after what happened and all..."

"Listen, Ann—this ain't about sex or nothing. The block is hot, so all I'm trying to do is come over there with you and chill. We can just kick it and watch a movie or do whatever—all bullshit aside. You feel me?"

Pain knew Annette was uncomfortable, and as he talked he realized his cousin had really put him up on some good game—and in a way the situation made him feel bad, because he felt like he should've handled their first time in bed differently. Right now his goal was to convince her to let him come over, with no sexual intentions involved.

"Scott... I don't want you to feel bad about what happened between us or anything."

"Dammit, Annette—I don't feel bad about shit I do unless it's a mistake," Pain yelled, cutting her off. "Now all I'm trying to do is chill out with you on some real shit. You can either give me the directions or I can call my cousin and ask him—but how we play it is up to you."

Annette was shocked by Pain's anger—and it actually made her feel a mix of fear and excitement. No man had ever come at her like this, so it threw her off balance. All the fight went out of her because she knew he would really call Keith and ask how to get to her house. (What she didn't know was Keith would not have told his cousin; to him, that would've been disrespectful.) However, the pressure from Scott Baylor was enough to make her give him her information.

Chapter 17

Pain was carrying a liquor-store bag in one hand and a KFC bag in the other when he got out of the car at Annette's house. She answered at eleven o'clock, wearing a white robe over a white nightgown. There was no nervous moment for the young thug; he quickly made himself at home.

"Damn, babygirl—I see you were ready to go to bed, for real."

"Yes, Pain. I told you I was."

"Well, shit—it's cool though. Look, Ann, why don't you step into the kitchen and grab some glasses and some ice? I need to grab the movie I left in the car, okay?"

"Okay, Scott," Annette replied as she got up from the sofa.

When she came out of the kitchen with the glasses, Pain was already in front of the television putting in a DVD. She took a seat on the living-room sofa. Once he had the movie rolling, Pain sat down beside her—removing a very large gun from his waist and placing it on the coffee table—then mixed them both glasses of Frïs Vodka with Ruby Red grapefruit. He noticed Annette had gone completely quiet.

"Yo, babygirl—you all right?"

"No. I mean—uh, Scott... Pain, why do you have that?"

"Oh, hush, Ann. That's my best friend—this .357 right here. I'm never one to go around without my piece, you feel me? But just chill, babygirl—you straight," Pain said, passing Annette a glass of his favorite mix.

"Okay, Pain, I guess so... but what we watching?"

"Oh, I got that Hellboy joint—so I hope that's cool."

"Yes—that's fine. I haven't seen it."

After forty-five minutes, Annette was fast asleep in Pain's lap while he kept watching the movie. This was the first time anything like this had happened to either of them, and Scott kind of thought it was cool. Soon he rolled a blunt and set it by him. He let the movie play without waking her, enjoying the relaxed feeling. The soft thug wasn't even aware his fingers were slowly running back and forth through Annette's hair. Time ticked by before Pain found himself dozing on the sofa as well. It was 2:00 a.m. when they woke up, and about 2:15 when the two of them decided to get a room.

—

"Yo, Keith—I got a play set up and I need you to be my quarterback," Babyboy said into his cell.

"I hear you, Baby—so what's the scenario before I come into the game?" Keith asked.

"Oh, we down by Hastings, so we heading into the fourth—but these white boys can play." (Translation for the uninitiated: he had a customer in need of a half-ounce, and the coded talk kept specifics off the phone. Real hunters understand the language that thugs communicate with.)

"Say, Babyboy—I'm getting off the expressway. Is the camp full?" Keith asked as he exited I-285.

"Yeah, dog—that spot jumping tonight, so just swing on in," Babyboy said.

Keith parked at the gas dump and walked in; Babyboy came in seconds later. One way of making a small drug transaction is to meet up on a produce line, give your partner some dap, and keep walking. That was called old-schooling; it only works where the two people involved can truly trust each other. As the two men shook hands, the money and the drugs were exchanged in the same motion. Keith went to the register, paid for $120 worth of gas, and left.

"That was fast, boy," Roselyn said as Keith was pulling off.

"Yep—but try to remember I'm dealing with family, so I'm not hanging around waiting on whoever wants that shit, babydoll. Here—do me a favor and count this," Keith said, reaching into his coat pocket and handing Rose a roll of bills.

"Damn, baby—this is four hundred dollars. You just made four hundred dollars in, what—two or three minutes?" Rose said, counting the money a second time.

Keith looked over at Rose and fell out laughing.

Too many people get tricked into the game because of the illusion—a complete misconception of how that business really works. It's one reason doing dirt has become so dirty: too many people with no business in that life make the choice to get involved.

"Listen, Rose—you my baby, so I'm gonna say this and hopefully you won't take it the wrong way. If every move I made was that easy and simple, nobody would waste time going to school or doing the right thing. On most days I gotta hump like a motherfucker just to make two hundred dollars—so don't get tricked by what you might see from the sidelines, baby."

"But Keith—I've watched you pick up money once before, and it didn't look all that hard."

For a few minutes Keith didn't say a word as he thought over what she'd said. Now, he figured, was the time to get Roselyn to understand a couple things about his life as a hustler.

Chapter 18

"Rose—the street life is full of snake motherfuckers," Keith began, a steel edge in his voice. "Brothers in the game often come face to face with a whole range of problems, baby. You can do business in Herndon Homes, Kimberly Courts, or Vine City for twenty years, and every motherfucking hustler out there with you can be on some kind of slime shit. Hell, baby—your own brother might just up and try you on some fuck shit."

"But Keith, baby—if the life of a hustler is so shady, why do you even take the risk?" Roselyn asked, completely caught up in what her man was saying.

"Well, to be honest—I'm just trying to pay my bills and live decent. Other people got a whole list of reasons. Don't get me wrong—I'd like to make that one major move and be able to say 'fuck this shit.' But, baby, most folks in the game have never had a kilo—let alone seen one."

"Hold up, now, Keith. Nah—I can go down a list of different rappers as well as book writers who talk about being in the drug game—"

As soon as Roselyn made that statement, Keith roared with laughter—because once again a misconception was front and center. It was a while before he could fully regain control and pick up where he left off.

"Babygirl—let me give you some game, for real. Forty-five percent of those cats who write books or rap on a record don't know shit about this life. Every once in a while a player comes along who has a little knowledge—but that motherfucker is one out of a thousand. Look, Rose—just think about this for a minute, seriously. If selling drugs and hustling was so easy, why aren't there more dope dealers and hustlers than people going to work every day?"

The question truly gave Roselyn something to think on; it was serious. Roselyn and Keith parted company at 2:30 in the morning—which just so happened to be when Annette and Pain were experiencing their second sexual encounter.

Rose's Cadillac needed brake work, so she left with the keys to Keith's Chrysler 300. As she was driving off, the sound of Anthony Hamilton's "Charlene" was playing loud from her car speakers.

***

"Motherfucker—lay down! You know what it is," Pain roared, coming into the hotel room. "Yo, B-Man—tie that bitch nigga up," he ordered Babyboy, his partner in crime.

While Babyboy did as instructed, Pain's cell rang.

"Run your mouth," he answered.

"Yo, cuz—we need to meet up," Keith said.

"I hear you, playboy—but check it, I'm a little busy at the moment. Let me hit you back."

"That's cool, cuz. Be safe."

"No doubt, playboy—no doubt," Scott said, hanging up.

—

It was the next day, and Keith was getting ready for work. When he woke up, he had his cousin on his mind heavy, so he gave him a call—unaware of what Pain had been doing at that exact moment the night before.

Babyboy had been in the Blazing Saddle talking to a dancer named Tasty when the same brother they were now robbing came under his radar. Hot Chocolate, SoBlack, and another sister were having problems with the dude, and Babyboy knew the club's bouncers were about to throw him out with a real beatdown. Sure enough, ten minutes later the dude was catching a fresh issue from the muscle men, and that's when Babyboy rushed outside to his car.

It was 2:45 in the morning when he made it to the Red Carpet Inn behind the clown (as he'd labeled their victim). Watching to see which room the man went into, Babyboy was forced to make a hard decision: he could rob the dude by himself and only get what was in his pockets, or he could sit still and wait until Pain was up and moving—then they could strip the clown for every single penny.

Sometimes waiting pays off in a big way, or it makes you miss out. The robbery went down without a problem, and the two men soon left with $1,800 in cash and two ounces of butter. Robbing, jacking, playing the pistol game can be just as addictive as smoking crack. With each small victory the robber gets bolder and more daring—and Babyboy, along with his road dawg, were about to find out that no addiction is easy to beat.

Chapter 19

"Nique, are you busy?"

"Nope. I can talk while I work."

"You're still at work? Baby, it's after six o'clock."

"Oh damn, Poochie—my fault. I'm changing the brakes on Roselyn's car."

"Ah, so you at Keith's house?"

"Yes, Stacey, I'm at Keith's house. I am on the ground, under a car, and working. Do you have any more questions, Miss Nosey?"

"No, Mr. Smarty—but you know that working men turn me on."

"Oooh—shit!" Q exclaimed, bumping his head. "Damn, Poochie, you made me hit my head."

He could hear Stacey giggling, which made him laugh too. She was at home taking a bath and, sitting in the tub, decided to give him a call.

"You know I'm gonna get you back, right?"

"Ooh, poor baby, I'm so sorry. Can I come make it up to you?"

"Yes, you can come—but I plan on making you suffer," Nique said, smiling.

"Is that a promise, Q?"

"I'll even offer you a generous deal if you can get here in the next hour."

"Do I get to hear what this generous deal consists of?" Stacey replied, sitting up in the tub.

"Nope. You gotta put up or shut up."

"Oh, that's a challenge, mister. Now it's on. Bye!" Poochie exclaimed, laughing as she hopped out of the bathtub.

Nique was done with Roselyn's car by the time Stacey got there, and once again they had his house completely to themselves—Keith was at work. A stress-free relationship is pretty much make-believe, but in the case of Nique and Poochie that's exactly what it was: stress-free. Some might say it was because Q wasn't a full-time hustler. Others might say it was because neither Stacey nor Q was pressing the other about titles. They were two people who chose to enjoy each other with no demands—pure and simple.

"Hey—say, Keith, ain't that your ride pulling in?" Babyboy asked, passing a blunt to Pain in the back seat.

"Yeah, dog, that looks like Rose—and Annette riding shotgun," Pain said, still counting money.

Keith's purpose for coming to the block tonight was to pick up the money the two men owed him. His game plan was to pay SoBlack back the next day so he'd have her out of his pockets. He'd already flipped the three grand twice in the past five days, so things were looking a little better for the home team.

As Babyboy handed him thirteen hundred, Pain passed his cousin two grand more from the back seat. Roselyn was parking beside Keith's 300; he got out, walked around to the passenger side, and Annette got out and slid into the driver's seat of the Camry. Babyboy dipped to run down a customer and Pain got into the front seat with Annette.

"Rose, baby—turn a block or something so I can count this paper."

"Okay, no problem. Let me tell Ann to follow us real quick," Roselyn said, letting down the window.

The two cars drove off and ended up parking in the Home Depot lot. Keith sat on the passenger side counting—his total was forty-five hundred. After doing the math in his head, he realized he'd still have sixty-two hundred of his own money even after paying SoBlack her money back.

"Roselyn, baby—don't take this the wrong way, but I don't want you driving this car to the block again."

"Keith, where the hell did that come from?" Rose shot back, a little attitude rising.

"It comes from the fact nobody—other than my folks—knows I even have this car. It also comes from the fact this car is in my grandmother's name, and I give her the money to pay the note, Rose."

"Okay, baby—I can understand that. Now tell me, are we going out tomorrow night or what?"

"Rose, I have to work tomorrow night from six till midnight, so you'll have to take that trip without me."

"But, Keith, baby—if you get off at twelve we can still go out."

"No, we can't, Roselyn, because I have some business to handle when I get off."

"Oh, now, Mr. Baylor—what business do you need to handle that's more important to you than me?"

There was no question Rose was losing her temper—and mainly because she wanted her way. Keith would risk his life for his woman, but with him it was business first, pleasure second.

"Baby, listen. I need to pay a friend of mine some money back that I borrowed, so I'll have to make it up to you."

"And you better not think that you won't, either," Rose said with a devilish smile.

Rose drove Keith to his spot, followed by Annette and Pain in the Camry. The two couples hung out at his spot laughing and talking trash for two hours before Pain needed to go back to the block and Roselyn had to take Annette home.

Society stays confused about how hustlers live on a daily basis, because what really happens compared to what you see on TV is totally different. The day for a hustler has to be thought out like the day for the owner of a pizza spot—and the boss or manager has to make quick adjustments for everything that isn't in the plan.

Chapter 20

"Rene, what time is your man coming through, girl?"

"Priscilla, girl—I told your good, dust-snorting ass: 12:30. Now stop getting on my damn nerves. Hell, you lucky I even called him for no damn $500 bag of soft."

"Hush, girl, please! You know damn well money talks. And my—well—gets wet too, shit. Act like you said something."

"Chile—hit! Keith just pulled up," Rene said, looking out of the apartment window. "Girl, come on with that little money so I can handle that lil' business real quick."

"Damn, Rene—I can take care of my own business, shit. And, bitch, you can call somebody else to deal with your bullshit, too. Now, cough up that little change or go cop your poison elsewhere!"

Priscilla knew Rene was dead serious—but damn, she didn't have to be so nasty. Every since this hoe got to fucking with a baller, she'd been forcing her damn place. One day, bitch, your ass gonna fall off that high horse. You just wait, Priscilla thought, pulling the money out of her bra. When Rene went out the door she mumbled, "Bitch, your ass better hope that nigga don't find out you been stealing from him."

Rene never heard a word—she was rushing to see him.

Keith was driving Roselyn's Cadillac because he wanted to test the brakes before she got it back. He was on his cell when Rene got in on the passenger side, so he just reached into his right jacket pocket and gave her a large Ziploc bag. Rene was counting money when Keith hung up, so he patiently waited for her to finish before he said a word.

"Baby, I need to go by the room before it gets too late. Oh—and here is $730. Check. Listen—everything is mixed up in that bag, so you can give Priscilla her shit out of there," Keith said as he counted the bills.

"Rene, can you wait till I go change before I take you to the room?"

"Baby, that's cool. That way I can catch a few more sells before it starts slowing down."

"Cool, baby. Listen—I gotta roll, so let a bigga nigga get a kiss or something before I bounce."

The sound of Ginuwine's "In Those Jeans" pounded out of the Cadillac as Keith pulled off. Rene put a little more twist in her hips as she walked back to Priscilla's apartment. No question—Rene was a ghetto dime piece, and Keith just shook his head and laughed as he drove.

Unfortunately, her mind was stuck on "fast" and that was her feeling on the good-life, period. Too many hustlers fall in love with females like Rene and come out on the losing end. All it takes is a brother to get locked down and his shit starts to disappear at record-breaking speed. Those were the thoughts shooting through his mind as Keith drove off.

When he got to the apartments' exit, an Atlanta police car was driving in. The two officers gave Keith a hard, measuring look as they passed, and Keith gave them a hard look back before driving into traffic.

"Well—time to change cars before coming back out. No sense making the pigs' work easy," Keith thought to himself, smiling.

***

"Hey, Blackgirl—your man is out there!" Tasty yelled as she walked into the dressing room.

"My man?" SoBlack replied, confused.

"Yes, girl—that fine ass Keith Baylor," Tasty exclaimed.

Immediately three more strippers started asking Tasty questions like: "Any other members of the Baylor boys out there?"

and "Did he get a dance before you came back?" Their excitement only made SoBlack smile—because the chances of any of these hoes fucking with Mr. Keith Baylor was a big fat zero.

Tameka put on the finishing touches before being announced to go on stage. Jodeci's "Feenin'" was the music she performed her set to, and she completely captivated every eyeball inside the Blazing Saddle. Keith was totally mesmerized looking at the beautiful Black sister—and she never took her eyes away from his as she put her heart and soul into her performance. To say SoBlack was amazing would be an understatement. Keith's mouth went dry as he watched this woman—this damn goddess—enthrall her audience. By the time the show was over, he couldn't help but notice he had a hard-on from hell—and it had Tameka "SoBlack" Perry's name written all over it.

Chapter 21

"All right, B-Man—on the count of three, kick in the damn door," Pain whispered.

Babyboy's only response was a nod of his head as he stood on the opposite side of the motel-room door. Once again the partners in crime were up to no good—this time at a rundown motel on Fulton Industrial. They were acting off a tip for this lick—a bad decision without doing any homework on the intended victim.

On the count of three, using his fingers, Babyboy—boom!—Room 201 was kicked in and the two men rushed in... to be greeted by an empty motel room.

"What the fuck—" Pain said, confused, dumb look on his face.

"Man, cuz—ain't no motherfucking body in this bitch," Babyboy replied, coming out of the bathroom.

"I know that, B-Man. Shit—maybe we hit the wrong damn room," Pain said, thinking fast and looking around the two-bed room. "Shit! Shit! Shit! Cuz, we just went on a dummy mission. Fuck, cuz—I hate damn dummy missions. Somebody has to pay for this bullshit!"

Babyboy waved his gun. Pain slid his pistol into the back of his pants. "Calm down, dog—let me think."

They were so caught up that it took them off guard when the manager spoke from the doorway. It played like a scene out of a comedy movie, the way the two men jumped when they heard the Asian's voice.

"Hey, you—mother bitch! Hey! Fuck door! You fuck door, bitch!" yelled the small man, turning darker with each word.

Well—something is better than nothing. That was the look shared by Babyboy and Pain. Scott Baylor's reaction caught the manager by surprise; the man had never been robbed before. Pain rushed the much smaller man quicker than you could say "what," cracked him with a hard right to the chin, and before he hit the ground the robbers were carrying him into the bathroom. Quickly they stripped their victim down to his birthday suit, leaving him out cold in the tub. Time wasn't on their side, so they rushed out to the car and away from Fulton Industrial—few dollars richer and too mad to laugh about what had just happened. At that moment, at least.

***

Back on Jonesboro Road, Pain and Babyboy were drinking Frïs Vodka and smoking a blunt, finally laughing over the fiasco. It was late—customers were either out of money or taking a break from getting high.

"Yo, cuz—did you see how the Chinaman was jumping around, cursing and shit?" Babyboy laughed.

"Hell yeah, cuz! 'Fuck door, fuck door!'" Pain roared, tears rolling down his face. "But damn, cuz—you went and knocked Jackie Chan's ass out, dog. Now that was some beautiful shit, P."

"No doubt, Babyboy. No doubt," Pain said, still chuckling. "Damn, P—there's your girl, dude."

"Fuck. Babyboy, I know. I told Annette not to be popping up out here and shit—damn."

Annette parked in front of the pay phones because she wasn't sure what to do as she pulled into the gas station. She didn't have to worry about deciding—Pain made the choice for her.

"Cuz, turn a block or two and let me handle my shit with Ann real quick," Pain said, getting out of the car.

Annette didn't see him approaching, so she almost had a heart attack when he knocked on the passenger window.

"Boy, you almost scared me to death. You shouldn't frighten people like that," Annette said, holding her chest.

"Look, Ann—what did I tell you about coming to the block?" Pain asked, blowing weed smoke. "Hello to you too, Mister Baylor—damn."

"Fuck that hello shit, Annette! I don't play where I eat. I don't trick with no freaks. I was born hard—so do I look weak? What I tell you is what it is, Annette. I'm making myself clear to you."

Unprepared didn't begin to cover it; Annette was speechless. Minutes went by before another stunning moment: Pain took another slow pull from his blunt and, at the same time, grabbed Annette by her shirt collar and pulled her close. Blowing "dro" smoke into her face and slowly removing the blunt from his mouth with his right hand, he spoke.

"I am nothing like the other clowns you used to dealing with, Annette. If I tell you to shit on yourself—make no mistake about me meaning it. Now, since you want to kick it with an all-nighter nigga, I advise you to get ready to pull an all-nighter. Here—smoke this blunt. Let that seat back. If you need to pee-pee, let me know first."

For the remainder of the morning, Annette received a crash course in the thug life from her man, Scott "Pain" Baylor. It was 8:00 Saturday morning when they got to Annette's house, and 9:30 before she went to sleep. Pain made her take a hot shower when they came in while he made breakfast. When they finished eating, he wanted sex—the kind that starts in the kitchen and ends in the bedroom.

If Annette thought her "Friday from hell" was over, she was never more wrong—because Pain made her hang out with him again all night Saturday until 6:00 a.m. Sunday. It was his way of making sure she never again felt the urge to pop up on the block without asking him first.

Chapter 22

"Sometimes I wonder what things will be like when I'm fifty or sixty years old. I go to work, pay my bills—but I live in an apartment."

"Poochie, that's the same thing everybody is doing," Nique said. "Unless you're rich—and then you still work. You work at keeping it. Rich folks just have a different set of problems. They can choose what day of the week they feel like handling their business, or pay someone else to handle headaches for them."

"Well, baby, I can't argue there," Nique shrugged. "But I bet sometimes all that wealth is a pain in the ass."

"Hey there, you two lovebirds. What's up?" Roselyn said, greeting Stacey and Nique as she shrugged off her coat and sat down.

The crew was linking up at Applebee's on Memorial Drive. It had been a few days since Nique or Roselyn had seen Keith, and he was due to show up any minute.

"Roselyn, it's 8:30. Where the hell is Keith?" Nique asked, checking his watch.

"Oh, he said he should be here in about five minutes, Q. He's coming from somewhere off Covington Highway."

Nique didn't get to ask another question—Keith came striding toward the table. After dapping his partner, giving Roselyn a light kiss on the cheek, and speaking to Poochie, the foursome skipped small talk. Nique signaled a waitress and everybody placed food and drink orders.

"Poochie, did you talk to Ann?"

"Yes—and before you ask, she's not coming."

"Well, why the hell not? That's what I'd like to know."

"Rose, don't start, okay?" Poochie said. "She's hanging out with Scott or something—that's all she'd tell me. Now please leave it alone, because whatever she's doing with him is her business."

"Well excuse me, Miss Poochie, for being concerned," Roselyn said, sticking out her tongue at her friend.

Nique and Keith exchanged a look that said, Don't comment. The two men stayed quiet while the women sparred.

"Q, what were you and Poochie talking about before I came up?" Keith asked.

"Nothing really—mainly getting old and how rich people's problems compare to regular working folks' problems."

"Yes—I'll bet you found out there's no comparison," Roselyn said.

"Wrong, Miss Smart-Pants," Stacey shot back. "Actually there are."

Truth be told, Poochie hadn't agreed with her man during their earlier discussion—but she knew it wouldn't take much to get Roselyn's blood pumping for a debate about the haves versus the have-nots.

"Wait a minute," Roselyn said, looking between the couple. "You mean to tell me you and Nique think rich people and working people have something in common?"

Keith took a sip of his drink and leaned back to enjoy the show. No way in hell was he hopping into a couples' debate—unless his boy and Stacey started to get the best of his girl. He smirked and listened.

"You see, Rose," Nique said, "like I told Stace—rich people have to get up and work the same as we do. The only difference is, they work at maintaining what they have. But I bet even that isn't easy."

"Okay, Q, I'll agree that far," Roselyn said, "but those same wealthy people can pay folks to take care of their business."

"Ha! That's the exact same thing I said," Poochie chimed in.

"Okay—now give up another comparison, Nique," Roselyn challenged. "Because I'm not buying this 'rich versus working class are on the same page' thing."

"Oh—so now y'all trying to gang up on a brother?" Nique grinned. "Look, all I'm saying is rich people have problems the same as we do. They pay taxes. They have insurance. They've got to eat and get rest like everybody else."

"Yes, but they can buy a bigger steak—or a new car instead of a used one," Poochie cut in, laughing behind her hand.

The debate was on: Poochie and Roselyn versus Nique. Keith wasn't about to let his boy stand alone without a fight, so he slid in.

"Hold up," Keith said. "Both of y'all can't turn this into a two-on-one on my partner. Let me tell you two sisters something."

"Give it to 'em, dog," Nique nodded.

"Check it out, ladies," Keith said. "The difference between rich and poor is largely an illusion. Don't get me wrong—everybody wants to be privileged and not worry about earning an income. But remember: the rich and the poor can't live without each other. If I own a hotel and nobody rents one of those rooms, all I've got is a piece of property."

"Yes, Keith, baby—but you have to have money in order to own that hotel," Roselyn said.

"You're correct, Rose, my love," Keith replied. "But I might not have as much money as you think. I could be leveraged to the ceiling—property rich, cash poor."

"Oh hell nah, Keith," Stacey said. "You can use that same hotel property to purchase another business."

"Yes, Stacey, I could—but then I'd have a whole 'nother gang of bills. My interest increases, my headaches increase, and it's all a gamble. People might not like my hotel. My rooms might never stay full."

"That's real shit, Q," Keith said, excited. "Which brings me back to what I said—being 'rich' is an illusion. What we're all really after are the privileges that well-off people enjoy."

Chapter 23

After the debate, conversation drifted to lighter topics. Near eleven, the gathering broke up. Roselyn followed Keith back toward the block on Jonesboro Road, leaving Stacey and Q in the Applebee's lot.

As Rose pulled into Memorial Drive traffic, she saw Poochie and Nique kissing by his car. Watching that scene for just a few seconds gave her a warm feeling that made her smile.

"Well, at least my girl is happy," she thought, dialing Annette as she slipped onto 285 behind Keith.

Two rings later, Annette picked up.

"Hey, girlfriend—where you at?" Rose asked.

"Rose, girl, I'm out here on the hottest street in Atlanta, watching my crazy-ass old man."

"Oh yeah? I hope you're being careful," Rose said, concern in her voice.

"Please, Rose—I'm fine. But girl, there ain't no way in hell I could sell drugs for a living."

"I heard that, Ann. Listen—I'm gonna talk to you in a few minutes. Tell me where you're parked."

***

"Yo, Keith, I need three grams of that softball, playboy!" Silk—the barber who cut hair inside the gas station—shouted from the door.

"I can do that, Silk, baby. Give me about ten, fifteen minutes at most and then we can play," Keith said at the pay phone, shaking the barber's hand as he passed.

Two minutes later Babyboy came strolling out of the 76, sipping a Fruit Punch and talking on his cell. He and Silk traded slight nods before the barber headed back inside. Once he was gone, Babyboy and Keith dapped up and hugged before getting to business.

"Babyboy—where the hell is Scott?"

"Oh, cuz is over there in the car with Ann."

"That's cool, I'll rap with him in a minute. So what's going on out here?"

"Shit, cuz—same ol' same. Twelve been riding a little, but not much since they busted that stupid bitch Moosey's house up the street."

"Bullshit."

"No, Keith, baby—real shit. Real talk. Check it—you know how that freaky bitch loves messing with them young lives. This dumb chick had Young Killa, Pumpkinhead, and Junebug's hot asses up in her crib."

"Ah, fuck, cuz—those dudes are as hot as a virgin in India. You damn right—key men. What happened?"

"Here's the beautiful part," Babyboy said dryly. "Pumpkinhead and Junebug's stupid asses robbed a cab driver at the stop sign at 8:30. Then they shot up into Moosey's house to chill."

"Oh, don't tell me, dog..."

"The cab driver saw where they went and told the po-po?"

"Hell nah, cuz—the cabbie saw Junebug smoking a blunt in the front yard of Moosey's house."

"Well, we won't be seeing those fools for a minute."

"At least Young Killa didn't get caught up—"

"Wrong again, cuz," Babyboy cut in. "Damn, your average is shitty tonight. Look—every single person in Moosey's house went to jail. Everybody."

"Damn," Keith said, lighting a Newport. He kept one fact to himself: it was a $1,500 hit. He'd just fronted Young Killa,

Pumpkinhead, and Junebug a $500 bundle of crack apiece. A loss he couldn't afford—and not a damn thing he could do about it. Now he had to figure out a way to make up nine hundred of it quick, and that was part of the game: make up for losses as fast as you learn about them, or end up broke. Sometimes losses were small enough to shrug off; sometimes they were big enough to damn near break you.

Keith's thoughts were racing a thousand miles a minute when Pain walked up, forcing him to put the $1,500 problem on hold—for now.

***

"Hey, Rose. B—" Annette started as she slid into the passenger seat.

"Ann, since when did you pick up a new occupation?" Roselyn asked.

"Oh, shit, girl—you know I ain't selling no damn drugs."

"Maybe not, but you sure as hell smell like a marijuana plant."

"Rose, don't start no shit. Will you go up the street to Mickey D's? I'm hungry as hell."

Rose used every ounce of self-control to not argue, started the car, and pulled off. Driving the short distance to McDonald's, she glanced at her friend, who looked like she hadn't slept in a week.

"Ann—are you trying to prove a point or something?"

"What do you mean, Rose? Prove a point to who?"

"Annette, we're friends, so don't take this the wrong way. Maybe you're trying to show Scott how down you are by hanging out while he does his thing, or whatever..."

Rose rolled through the drive-thru, putting Annette's response on hold while she ordered food. Once their order was in, the conversation resumed.

"Roselyn, I've been out here with Scott the last two nights in a row," Annette said. "And if it makes you feel any better, I told him this would be my last night. When I came out here it was really to see my man and just kick it. I honestly didn't have a clue about all the things drug dealers go through—and it's crazy. A person would have to be nuts to live that kind of life. I can tell you, girl, that I couldn't."

During Annette's soul-baring speech, Rose never said a word—she just listened, sensing that Ann needed to talk. She was happy to hear her best friend wasn't going to be running around in a thugged-out element any longer. The truth was Annette was out of her depth. At least she'd learned it without something bad happening first.

If only Annette and Roselyn knew—this was exactly what Scott was doing by dragging Ann out to the block each night. He was stripping away every misconception in her mind about the street life. Had he heard the conversation between the two friends, he'd have smiled and said, Mission accomplished.

Chapter 24

"Renee! Renee—guess what, girl!" shouted Latrell, a dark-skinned powder-head who changed sleeping partners like stockings.

"What, Trell? I'm busy," Renee replied, counting bags of drugs on the living-room table.

"Girl, they just busted Moosey's house—and took all they stupid asses to jail."

That was enough to make Renee stop what she was doing and give her gossiping friend full attention.

"Trell, who all went to jail at Moosey's house?"

"Moosey, Young Killa, Pumpkinhead, and Junebug. Lawanna told me Pumpkinhead and Junebug robbed a cab driver or some stupid shit. I was coming out of the 76 with Rowda when I heard Babyboy telling Keith about it."

"Damn—that's some fucked-up shit, Trell."

"Yeah, I knew it. But Pain told me Keith was going by the jail tomorrow and leaving all four of them a little money."

"My man is crazy," Renee snapped. "If I was his ass I wouldn't take their dumb asses shit."

"Girl, you can't be that way," Trell said. "Moosey and Young Killa didn't rob nobody, Renee—and it ain't no telling how long they'll be locked up before they come out of that garbage."

"Whatever, Trell. To me, triflin' people deserve to have stupid shit happen to them," Renee said, going back to counting product.

Cutting someone else down—if not physically, then verbally—is human nature. Today's word for it is "hating." No matter who you are—a homeless person or a Fortune-500 CEO—for every ten people who support you, ten will dislike you. A hundred people can walk by that homeless person and never know they were rich once. The folks angry about the CEO's success don't know how hard he or she worked to get there.

Renee could care less about anyone else—and that included Keith to a degree. He represented a status statement to her. If he fell tomorrow, she'd grab hold of the next baller.

***

"Do you feel up to going out tonight?" Roselyn asked as she came out of the bathroom from taking a shower.

"Going out where, baby? It's Monday—not exactly club night," Keith said, lying in Roselyn's bed.

Rose had come home from work to find Keith dead asleep at 5:30 in the evening. It was a temptation she couldn't resist—first time she'd ever come home to a greeting that delicious. There was a part of her that considered not waking him, but her thoughts of pleasure drowned out her logic. She slipped off her shoes, slid into the bed, and climbed over to him. Keith, asleep on his stomach, had no idea she was there until she was on his back, kissing his neck and moving up to his ear. A deep growl seeped from his half-sleep throat, and for the next forty minutes Roselyn controlled the tempo of their private contest.

"Keith, we don't have to go to a club to go somewhere," she murmured afterward. "We can just hang out together like we used to."

"Baby, you making this sound like we never see each other or go anyplace together."

"I don't mean it like that, Keith. I'd just like to do something with my man tonight. Is there something wrong with that?"

"No, Roselyn—there ain't nothing wrong with that, and I never said there was. So don't go getting defensive. But I do want you to know you're asking us to go out on Monday—which is my first off-day."

"What the hell? If you don't want to do shit with me, Keith, then just say so—but don't use this being your first day off as a damn excuse."

"Fuck, Rose—I didn't think what I said was an excuse. And where is that bullshit coming from about me not wanting to go anywhere with you?"

"I don't know, Mister Baylor—maybe I'm just hearing things that sound like excuses to me. I mean, do you have something else to do—or some other female you need to see, or what?"

That was enough to make an already heated Keith sit straight up in bed. If Roselyn thought he was hot before, she could see steam now.

"First off—if you want to ask me something about my business, another female, or anything else—just ask me," he said, eyes hard. "Second, I had shit to do before you and I were together, and I'm not doing anything new or different now. Third—don't ever imply a fucking thing, because then I might just give you the correct information, and you may not be able to handle it."

"Oh—so now I'm a little girl who needs you to filter my shit for me?"

"No, Roselyn—you're not. But you sure as hell are making me look at you like one."

"Fuck you, Keith!" Roselyn screamed.

Keith just gave her a hard look, got out of bed, and walked into the bathroom to take a shower. When he was done and fully dressed in the clothes he'd worn the night before, he walked out of Roselyn's place without looking back or saying a word.

What Roselyn didn't know was that Keith had come to her house for a little peace and comfort—not an argument. In the last three days he'd taken over three thousand dollars in losses, and because he had to be at work there was no way for him to correct the money loss or everything else that was going wrong. If this was any indication of how his day was about to be, then Keith Baylor had just received his first warning.

Chapter 25

"Seven, eight, nine, ten," Nique counted the reps as Keith racked the bar.

"Your turn, Q, dog." Keith rubbed his arms and slid off the bench. "Damn, my arms are burning."

It was their Monday-night routine at Gold's Gym on Camp Creek Parkway, about thirty minutes in. They'd started late—Nique had to swing by his mother's, and Keith got caught up handling business. On top of that, his argument with Roselyn had thrown his day off balance, and that's exactly what they were talking about.

"Q, man, I just don't get it," Keith said while Nique lay back under 225. "Me and Roselyn were having a discussion, dog—and all hell broke loose. One minute she's talking about going out somewhere together. The next minute it's me not wanting to go anywhere with her. Then suddenly it's another woman. I was so pissed I couldn't even talk. I mean, Q, I'm still confused about the whole damn argument."

Nique pushed the weight up and down, listening while he got his reps. At ten, he guided the bar to the hooks, sat up, and gave his best friend a hard look before he said a word.

"Keith, you my boy—but either you're stupid or you're crazy," Nique said, standing. "And by the way—it's your turn."

Keith blinked. "Come on, man."

"You gotta remember," Nique went on, "Roselyn really doesn't have a clue about half the shit you're doing. Second, she's a woman who wants to spend time with her man—but your dumb ass treated the situation and the conversation all casual, like it was a topic to kick around."

"Clank." Keith put the bar back before hitting ten; Q's words smacked like a bat.

"Hot—fuck—dammit, Q! I'm not a mind reader," Keith snapped. "She made a comment, I made a comment. That wasn't supposed to lead to a damn argument."

"Correct, old buddy. Not to you," Nique said. "But women throw hints and tell us half of what's on their mind. We, on the other hand, gotta catch those hints and handle whatever's on their minds—real damn fast."

"Bullshit, Q. In that case brothers will never win—'cause nine times outta ten we guessing."

"Exactly, Keith," Nique said, deadpan. "But haven't you figured it out? It's not about being right—it's about being considerate about those hints. I bet you if your Black ass had said, 'Roselyn, we can hang for a few hours, but I need to take care of some very important business,' y'all wouldn't have even argued."

"Bullshit—'cause then she would've brought up some mess like my business is more important than her, or I can afford to take one day off from running the streets."

"Look, Keith—I'm on your side, okay? And I sure as hell don't have all the answers," Nique said. "But let me ask you a question. Do you love Roselyn?"

"Of course, Q. What kind of question is that?"

"I asked because only somebody you love—or care about—can make you mad for no serious reason."

"Yeah, Q, I hear you," Keith said, exhaling. "Like they say—nobody can hurt you like the person you love."

"Come on. We got thirty minutes to finish," Keith added after a beat.

"I hear you—but you owe five more reps. Make it ten for keeping me waiting," Nique grinned, watching his best friend lie back on the bench.

Sometimes it helps to use a close friend as a sounding board. The advice may not be what we want to hear, but it can still matter. Keith and Nique were closer than brothers and had faced hard times side by side. Where they differed wasn't just how they made their living—it was in how they handled the women they let close. Either way, they knew each other's secrets and trusted each other without question.

Chapter 26

When they finished at the gym and split up, life threw Keith another curve. A message waited on his voicemail—Renee saying she'd been robbed and everything was gone.

For twenty minutes he sat in his car in the lot, music low, thinking about his life. His total money-and-drug losses were now over five grand. Small to the rich; huge to a brother hustling his heart out trying to get ahead.

"Fuck. Fuck! Fuck!!!" Keith roared, pounding the steering wheel. No amount of rage could change the situation or make up for the losses. For a man who'd been through prison already, it was getting harder not to just say "fuck it" and do something stupid.

He drove aimlessly for an hour, replaying the last four days. He knew he needed to check on Renee, but he was mentally off-balance. Cruising down Candler Road, he thought about the old days—corridor bus rides to Coan Middle School, when life was as simple as a few dollars in his pocket and junk food in his backpack. Memories can be bittersweet. Merging onto I-20 West, his phone cut through the haze.

"Keith Baylor, are you so upset with me that you can't at least call?" Roselyn's voice came through first.

"Roselyn, I don't have the energy to argue. If that's why you called—"

"No, baby, wait," she cut in. "I didn't call to argue. I called because I had a bad feeling and had to check on you—and I'm glad I did, because you don't sound right. Now tell me what's wrong."

"Rose...I don't know where to begin. Today's been rough," he said. "I guess God looks after babies and fools. I know I ain't a baby, so I must be the damn fool."

Hearing the hurt and frustration in his voice wiped Roselyn's mind blank for a second—the pain was unexpected.

"Keith, you know you can talk to me about anything," she said. "Baby, maybe just talking about it will help."

Trying not to let the evil in his feelings take over, Keith took a slow breath. "Rose, the problems I'm fucked up over involve street shit—the kind of garbage I'd rather keep out of our relationship, you feel me?"

"How can you say that, Keith, when there's not a day you're not putting down some shady deal?" she asked softly. "How can you even say that?"

"Look, Rose—I been up front with you from day one because you're special and important to me. But there's some shit about the game you'd never understand."

"I won't pretend I know the ins and outs," she said, "but I can tell you this: if the things you're into cause you this much trouble, maybe it's time to choose something else."

"Yeah, Rose. I know," he said quietly. "Believe it or not, I'm thinking about it—real hard."

After the call, Keith decided to put off Renee's situation for a few hours and swung by the shop that moved most of his bootleg X-rated DVDs. On paper, all the property paperwork was fake—"More Hustle Incorporated," a shell. He never worried about taxes. The hair-supply storefront was leased by a brother he'd been locked up with. That little setup kept his head above water.

Or had.

He exited at Candler and Stone Mountain roads, mind sorting a to-do list. Pulling into the plaza, the first thing he clocked was how dark it was where the shop sat. He didn't bother with a space—it was 10:45 and the spot didn't close until 11:30. He curb-parked and got out.

Nothing could've prepared him for the sign: FOR SALE—LEASE OR RENT.

If anybody wondered how much more he could take, the ice finally cracked.

Keith pressed to the windows to peer inside. What he saw made the normally composed Keith Baylor sway. The building was empty—stripped—nothing of material value left.

“Motherfuck me,” he growled—and whether it was fate or magic, who knows. By his left foot sat a red clay brick. Keith picked it up and launched it through the biggest window. Glass exploded across the tile like ice.

Chapter 27

A whole week went by without Keith seeing or speaking to a soul. As close as he and Nique were, Q couldn't get through. Keith's voicemail said he'd be out of town for a few days.

He wasn't out of town—not even close. Truth was, Keith Baylor was isolating himself as much as possible to keep from killing somebody. Roselyn sensed he was trying to protect himself the only way he knew how but didn't fully agree with how he was doing it.

Once he calmed down some, Keith checked on Renee and got the lowdown on the robbery. It wasn't clear who left the apartment's back door unlocked. Renee said she'd been asleep on the sofa when—suddenly—three men in ski masks with guns were standing around the living room. At first Keith thought she might be lying—he replayed her message over and over. But once he saw how shaken she was, there was no question she was telling the truth. He moved her somewhere safe until he could decide the next best move.

For the time being, Keith was resting his mind, body, and spirit at SoBlack's place—mainly because it was one of the few spots he had real peace, and no soul knew he was holed up there. At night he went to work; during the day, he slept in Tameka's bed. She gave him whatever he needed to get back on track. Pride can make us choose dumb options—Keith refused to borrow money from Tameka a second time. He was determined to fix his business issues on his own.

"Welcome to Car Titles for Cash, Mr. Baylor. I'm Clinton Frasier. You spoke with my supervisor, Ted Bailey, this morning. Please, have a seat."

"Thanks, Mr. Frasier. I appreciate you seeing me."

"No problem—that's what we're here for. Let's talk business. What amount are you looking to obtain against your vehicle?"

"Well, Mr. Frasier, somewhere around twenty-five hundred—at least."

"Keith—can I call you Keith?"

"Yeah, that's cool."

"Twenty-five hundred isn't a problem. What year is the car in question?"

"My Camry's a '98."

"Good. Are you in full ownership? We can't proceed if you're paying a note."

"Your guy told me that on the phone, so I brought my Camry instead of the Chrysler 300."

"Good—let's step out and take a look before we go any further."

In the parking lot, Frasier went over the car with a fine-tooth comb, checked the miles, snapped a few pictures—precautions in case the title-pawn went bad and Keith failed to pay back the borrowed money plus interest. The whole transaction took a little over a half hour. Keith left with a $2,500 check in his pocket—and a sour taste in his mouth about the whole thing. He was determined to pay the pawn back and unfuck his business.

First order of getting his game back on track: turn the check into cash, then purchase as much dope and weed as he could for the $2,500 he was now worth.

As he parked at the bank, SoBlack called.

"Run your mouth, Tam—I hear you," Keith answered.

"Okay, baby. How'd everything go?"

"It's all good, Blackgirl. I'm just trying to shake off the thought of pawning the title to my shit, you know?"

"Keith, baby—I told you you could've borrowed whatever you needed from me. You didn't have to—"

"Yeah, yeah, Tam, I know. But check it—that conversation is done. Let's not go back in that direction, okay?"

"All right, Keith. Well, listen—I'm about to stop by my mother's and then grocery shopping. Want me to get you anything while I'm running around?"

"Nah, babygirl, I'm cool. Let me run in the bank real quick. I'll call you later on when things slow down for me some."

"Okay, baby—be careful."

"Yeah, Tam. You too."

Tameka knew it might be a few days before she heard from him again. Truth be told, she'd called to hear his voice, not just to check in. The past week had grown on the sister quick. Coming straight home to sleep in the bed all day with Keith felt like new heaven. Commitment had never tugged like this. She was wrestling with whether to ask for one—because after the last week she felt in her heart this was the man she wanted to be with.

The only problem was Keith had so much noise running through his mind that nothing else could register. To him, he was fighting the hardest battle of his life—and losing was not an option. Maintaining his respect in the streets while taking care of business were the only important things to Keith Baylor at the moment.

Chapter 28

"Blackgirl, what's happening, girl?"

"Hey, Tosha, Chantell—and don't you say shit to me, Mee-Mee. I'm still mad at your crazy ass."

Most of the dancers from The Blazing Saddle, the Crazy Horse, and DreamGirls went to the same hair salon. For some reason, Monday was extra busy at New Visions. Miss Lucy—everybody called her Momma—was one of the best stylists in Atlanta. Strippers, gangsters, dealers—everybody knew Momma.

Tameka wasn't really mad at Mee-Mee; the twenty-year-old even knew her big sister wasn't for real. Right now, every chair was full. Poison, Chantell, Mee-Mee, and SoBlack were waiting on different stylists. Only two nail techs were in, so the ladies had to wait on them too.

Chantell and Poison were bi friends who loved to smoke weed and snort monster-ass powder. It wasn't long before Poison slid a question Tameka's way.

"Hey, Blackgirl, is Keith handling business today?" Poison whispered.

"Poison, you know I don't get involved with Keith's business."

"Shit, Blackie, give me his number and I'll ask him then. Hook, bitch—don't play."

"Hold your damn horses," Tameka said, dialing.

Two rings later, SoBlack was live with Keith. It was 5:30 in the evening. He'd been running back and forth all over Atlanta all day. The four and a half ounces he'd bought at noon were almost gone; the half a pound was down to an ounce. He was on his way to make another move when Tameka called.

"Baby, you busy?"

"I got time for you, Tam. What's crackin'?"

"I'm good, but somebody wants a little something."

"Okay—and what kind of money they talking?"

"Hold on, baby—let me see... Baby, can you do half soft, half green?"

"Yes, Tam, that's not a problem."

"Okay, hold on," she said, covering the phone to confer with Poison. "All right, baby, here's the deal—nine hundred dollars. One is for the green, eight for the other."

"A'ight, Tam. Where I need to come?"

"Oh—damn, sorry, baby. I'm at New Visions in East Point."

"That the same salon you used to use?"

"Yeah, same place."

"Bet. I'll be there in about ten minutes," Keith said, and hung up.

He met his connect at the Chevron on Stanton Road, then headed to New Visions in Tri-City Plaza. Every head inside turned toward the glass as he swung the 300 into the lot, bass thumping hard enough to rattle the windows. If folks thought they were ready to see the hard-knock hustler in person, they were in for a shock.

Keith Baylor stepped out in tailored black slacks, black gators, black shirt, black jacket. Dressed like that, every piece of jewelry looked bigger, brighter. He looked like money. Smelled like money. Had men and women double-taking as they passed. Today, Keith was projecting an energy that screamed, I am that motherfucker—and judging by the reaction, the statement landed.

SoBlack was flipping a hair-fashion magazine with Mee-Mee when he walked in carrying ten red roses with a single white rose in the center. Miss Lucy was first—one red rose for Momma. Then he worked the room, handing a red rose to every woman until only the lone white one remained. Tameka "SoBlack" Perry watched him circle the salon, feeling a little jealous of all the attention he was spreading—until he leaned down, kissed her light but powerful, and laid that single white rose in her hand. Time disappeared; so did jealousy.

There are men who hate a powerful personality. Some men have deep compassion for beautiful things mixed with a passionate love for people. Keith Baylor was one of those—and what made him dangerous to women was that nothing about him was fake. What made him a threat to men was that his natural habits were simply who he was. No games. No lies. The brother women loved and a lot of brothers hated—and he wasn't even aware.

***

"Yo, Keith, baby—where you at?"

"Shit, Q, I'm at the downtown section, doc. Over on Peachtree."

"Yeah, playboy—that's the spot. How long you gonna be there? I got a few people who wanna see your face."

"Swing through. It's cool. When you get here, come to the V.I.P."

"Look, dog, my pockets ain't in shape for that type of party."

"Q, don't worry about that—you know damn well I got you. I'll see you when you get here. One."

Keith was selling $25 bags of powder in V.I.P., and business was doing numbers. It was eleven o'clock and he was four grand thicker. Tomorrow he planned to knock down a chunk of house bills after seeing his parole officer.

At midnight, Nique, Stacey, Annette, and Roselyn joined him in V.I.P. Roselyn was caught off guard by how good her man looked in all black. Seeing him in this element, nobody would've guessed he was damn near flat broke twelve days ago.

"Damn, my baby is stunting on these fools," she thought, taking a seat.

"What's up, my G?" Keith hugged Nique and dapped him.

"Ain't shit, my man. Long time, no see," Q said.

"Yeah, dog, I know. Trust me. Ladies—will Grey Goose be too heavy, or what?" Keith grinned.

Once the bottle landed, he had to step away to handle business, then returned to find everyone laughing, drinking, easing into the night. Soon Roselyn was wrapped in his arms, trading small kisses, soaking in the moment. For two hours the crew did nothing but have a good time. Keith and Nique each hit the floor with one of the women, making it a truly good night for everybody.

Chapter 29

The next morning Keith sat at his kitchen counter sorting bills, counting out cash for each one, matching stacks to envelopes—when the doorbell rang. Roselyn had spent the night and left at 6:30 for home, then work. It was 8:15 a.m. He wasn't expecting company.

He peeped the peephole in boxers and ankle socks—and cussed under his breath. His parole officer stood there—with SoBlack right behind him, holding a Waffle House box.

"Shit."

He tiptoed back to stash the .380 he'd carried to the club, then opened up.

"Hello, Mr. Baylor. I was making a few house calls in the area, figured I'd stop by before I go back to the office."

"It's cool, Mr. Correll. Come on in. I'm sure you and Tameka have met."

"Yes, we have," Correll said. "Ms. Perry told me she was dropping by with breakfast, so we showed up at exactly the same time."

"Tam, you can go on back. Me and Mr. Correll shouldn't be long."

"Okay, baby. Nice to meet you, Mr. Correll," Tameka said, slipping to the bedroom.

Correll drifted through the living room into the kitchen—and stopped at the counter where Keith had left money mixed with bills.

"Well now, Mr. Baylor—that's a whole lot of cash for somebody making $7.50 an hour," Correll said, thumbing through both money and mail. "If I were a guessing man, I'd say you're into something very illegal."

"And if I was into something illegal, I'd be a fool to put it in your face, Mr. Correll," Keith shot back—pissed at himself for the dumb slip.

"Since I don't consider you stupid, I'll leave you with a piece of advice," Correll said. "Everything we do in the dark eventually comes to the light. And if it comes to the light, Mr. Baylor, my job is to send you back to prison."

"That some kind of threat?"

"No, Keith. A promise. If you screw up, I'll screw you—without thinking twice."

When Correll left, Keith was shook. Any appetite he had vanished with that house call. People on parole get told their PO is their best friend and counselor. Most find out the hard way that what they really have is their very own police officer—and 95% of the time, nothing you do is right. The PO sits patient for that beautiful "no-no," and the reason doesn't matter.

"Baby, you all right?" Tameka asked when he came to the bedroom.

"Yeah, Tam. Cool—just a little shook up," he said, sitting on the bed. "Damn, I can't believe I slipped like that. Now I gotta worry about that peckerwood breathing down my neck."

"Tam, since when you start popping up at my house?" he added, trying to change the feeling.

"Since you forgot to come by the club and pick up your money."

"What damn money, babygirl? I don't remember needing to pick up any bread."

She could tell he truly had no clue what she meant. Looking closer at him, Tameka also saw how exhausted he was.

"Keith, you need to be in bed, baby."

"I'll sleep when I'm dead. Now—what money are you talking about?"

"I'm talking about the nine hundred dollars from Poison and Chantell. You remember yesterday—New Visions—Keith Baylor passing out roses?"

"Oh... shit, Tam. My fault, girl. Damn, I forgot about that."

With New Visions crowded up, she'd walked outside with him to the car. It wouldn't have looked right for him to walk back in, so he gave SoBlack the product and left her to handle the transaction.

"Keith, baby—when's the last time you been to bed?"

"Shit, Tam, I don't have to sleep. I might've slept three hours since Sunday."

"Dammit, Keith Baylor—it's Tuesday."

"Tell that to my bills, 'cause they sure don't care about me going to sleep."

"Okay, baby—let's make a deal," Tameka said, easing his head into her lap.

"All right, Tam—I'm listening," he mumbled, settling in.

"How about I take care of those bills for you while you relax and get some sleep? I can do that. But let me ask you a question, Mr. Baylor."

"Shoot, Ms. Perry."

"Do I get some when you wake up?"

"Oh, I don't know... maybe—if you've slept your way into enough energy."

She didn't even need to answer. He was already out—head heavy in her lap. An hour later, Tameka slid from under him, grabbed her purse and keys, and went on a mission to handle his business.

What Keith didn't know was that Tameka went and paid every single bill—including the note on his 300.

Chapter 30

"Man, Pain—look at that sucker Cap," Babyboy said from their usual spot on the block. "Dude really think he pimpin' with his duck-walkin' ass."

"B-Man, I ain't even trying to see that clown," Pain said, pulling from a blunt. "My mind on some serious money-getting shit, doc."

"Look, P, ain't shit jumping off around here, man—unless you wanna call Keith and see what's crackin'."

"Nah, doc. My peeps ain't in position for the kind of action me and you need."

"I feel you, P. So what's on the menu then?"

"Give me a minute and I'll think of something..."

It was late Tuesday sliding into early Wednesday. Traffic on Jonesboro Road stayed moving, but customers were thin. Pain and Babyboy were juggling scraps compared to normal—partly because both had money-management issues. Scott's closet looked like a small Foot Locker—that's where his chunks of money went. Babyboy's woman was a vampire, sucking his cash as fast as he made it. They had other vices too: weed, liquor, and sometimes a couple pills of X. Truth was, they should've been mad at themselves, but it didn't feel like that. Things just weren't taking off fast enough, and with Keith not able to fatten their pockets like usual, frustration stayed high.

"Give me about twenty minutes, Renee, and I'll be there, okay?" Keith said into his cell as he slid into his Camry.

He was leaving Roselyn's, headed to see a customer wanting a $50 bag of powder. He'd woken at 5:30 Tuesday evening to find Tameka sleeping softly beside him and a full voicemail on his phone. After a good round of heated sex with the little goddess and grabbing something to eat, Keith gave SoBlack $1,800 to drop in her bank, promising more later. As soon as she left, he returned every call, showered hot, and hit traffic.

Business was a whole lot slower than the day before. He scooped Renee and Precious and went to the block. At ten o'clock, Roselyn was demanding a little attention, so he left the two women on the set with $200 worth of his product. Slow night—so the hard-knock hustler gambled small.

What he wasn't expecting was what he saw when he came back to pick them up.

"Hey—say, Renee, Precious, how about y'all get in the car so I can leave," Keith called from the driver's window, headlights flashing as he rolled up to the pumps.

Five minutes ticked by with both Renee and Precious paying attention to everything but Keith. He finally roared through the window, snapping them to the car.

"What the fuck is the problem, Renee?" he barked as soon as the doors shut.

"Oh, baby—I'm sorry, but your cousin them is trippin', Keith—look!" she said, pointing toward another pump.

Keith couldn't see what had her so excited, so he eased around to the other side of the station. Up close, it looked like Babyboy was lounging on the hood of a Honda while Pain leaned into the driver's window. To a casual passerby, nothing seemed wrong.

But looking harder, Keith saw it: his cousin was robbing the lady at the pump.

Mixed feelings ripped through him. Part of him wanted to interfere. Part of him told him it wasn't his business. While he sat there deciding, a Clayton County patrol car rolled into the station.

Keith just knew things were about to get ugly. He slid off, ready to be gone—only to see the officer make a U-turn and roll back out the entrance.

"Damn—some motherfuckers have all the luck," Keith said, gliding down Jonesboro Road.

Chapter 31

By the time Keith made it home sometime after 6 a.m., he was sleep on his feet. The night had been truly slow on the cash-flow end. He counted $685—everything he'd made.

"Damn... shit has to get better," he muttered, tossing the small pile of bills on his dresser and stripping off his clothes.

When he stepped out of the shower, the house phone started ringing. He flopped onto the bed, wrapped in a towel, and answered.

"Hello—Baylor residence."

"Good morning, boy."

"Hey, Roselyn, baby. What's up?"

"I'm about to go to work and felt like hearing your voice before I start my day."

"Oh, is that right?" Keith said, slow-rolling his words, one hand drifting.

"Yes, that's correct, Mr. Baylor. So tell me what your day's gonna consist of."

"Other than me fantasizing about you? Nothing much..."

That answer made Roselyn pause, sit on her bed, and smile like a little girl. She whispered into the phone, "Mr. Baylor, are you being bad over there?"

"That depends on what you call 'bad,' Ms. Moore."

"Keith, baby—don't do this to me, now."

"Do what?" he replied, breath thickening.

"Baby... can't you at least wait until I get off work?" she said, already getting turned on.

Sex over the phone was new to them. Roselyn was nervous and excited—and wet. Keith was more than ready to experiment.

"Rose, I know you only got on a bra and some panties. Lay back and picture me," he murmured, voice honeyed and heavy. Goosebumps rolled down Roselyn's body. With zero thought about "what's next," she found herself on her back, phone pressed to her ear, eyes closed, breath catching.

Being alone captures the heart, letting the two on the line act out feelings they don't say out loud. Keith and Roselyn made love over the phone, tightening their bond. Life was already complicated; a hustler's life even more so. What came next, nobody knew.

"Stacey, baby—what time did Keith say to meet at the skating rink?" Nique called from the bathroom.

"Oh, boy, we still got time. We don't have to be there until nine," Poochie said, laying jeans on the bed.

"Damn, can't believe I let Keith talk me into skating. I ain't skated since high school," Nique said, walking out, shaking his head.

"Don't worry. If you fall, I'm gonna be there to catch you, boo," Poochie teased.

The Friday-night idea was Annette's. The girlfriends had been hanging at Roselyn's, V-103 playing old school on the radio. When Soul Sonic Force's "Planet Rock" hit, the ladies were dancing and swapping memories. The talk slid to how fun skating used to be, and Annette started talking trash like Roselyn and Stacey couldn't skate no more. From there, it was on.

What they didn't know was that, at 8:05 p.m., a few more folks they knew were getting ready to join them at the rink, too.

Chapter 32

Friday nights at Sparkles Skating Rink weren't the younger crowd's night in Atlanta. Teen crews packed it on Saturdays and Sundays. Fridays were for the 30-and-over set—grown folks, couples, even families, enjoying a real vibe without the extra.

Keith, Roselyn, Nique, Poochie, Annette, Scott (Pain), Babyboy, and Babyboy's girl Michelle got to Sparkles almost the same time. Once the DJ dropped the old-school "Looking for the Perfect Beat," the skate show was on.

"Beep! Beep! Coming through! Player coming through!" Keith yelled, weaving between Poochie and Q, with Prin, Roselyn, and Annette in the line behind him.

"Yeah, a'right, player!" Nique hollered back, wobbling for balance, making Poochie laugh.

"Oh, baby, don't fall," she cried, grabbing his hand.

"I'm cool, Stacey. Just gotta get back used to this skating thing, that's all."

Three songs later, true to his word, Q was rolling smooth like everybody else. "Set It Off" pumped out the speakers and the whole crowd showed love. Folks not skating were dancing all around the rink. Babyboy and Michelle were the only couple not in skates, but they were still enjoying themselves. Soon the friends were snapping group pics and cracking jokes.

After leaving Sparkles, the eight slid to Riverdale for food at Denny's on Old National. A good night—one none of them would forget.

***

Ring, ring. "Hello," Keith answered.

"You have a collect call from... Renee. If you would like to accept the call, press 5."

It was 2 p.m. Saturday. Keith was home relaxing—he had to be at work at 10. Roselyn had just left for a hair appointment. He was in a good mood from their Friday-night skating run.

He pressed 5.

"Hey, Keith, baby—"

"Renee—why the hell you calling me from jail?"

"Keith, baby, I got locked up for having three counterfeit twenties this morning, 11:30. Baby, I need you to come get me—or give my sister the money."

"Renee, this a fucked-up time for you to be in damn jail. What jail are you even in?"

"I'm in Clayton County jail, Keith. My bond is eleven hundred, baby."

"Damn, Renee—so it'll be ten percent plus another hundred for security, right?"

"Yes, but they'll take $150 for my bond."

"Shit! Shit! Shit!" Keith snapped. "Out of all places, you had to get locked up in Clayton County. Listen—let me get dressed and go see your sister. All right?"

"Okay, baby. Thank you. I love you. Bye!"

"Yeah, you better," he muttered, hanging up.

He dialed the sister's number while heading to the bedroom. Three rings and another voice answered.

"Hey, this Keith. What's up, Miss Sexy? Lemme talk to Renee's sister—is this her?"

"No, baby, this is Renee's cousin, Angel."

"Okay, Angel—listen, I'm trying to see about getting your people out, so I need to talk to her sister."

"Keith, I know what's what. In fact, I'm the one posting the bond," Angel said.

"A'ight, Ms. Angel. What time can I bring you the money?"

"You can come by now, or call me when you're on the way."

Keith hesitated hard. He didn't know this woman, and the vibe she gave wasn't his favorite. Before getting off, he told her to meet him at the gas station at 7:30 so she could pick up the money.

"Yo, Babyboy—what's crackin'!" Keith yelled from his car after parking.

"Shit, playboy, I'm out here early because it's bill time. You feel me?" Babyboy said, hugging him.

"Yeah, dude, I feel you. That's why my Black ass is out here in my damn work clothes—I gotta grind and get Renee's crazy ass out of jail."

"Oh, shit—dog, for real? Damn, Keith—what she do?"

"Some crackhead paid Renee in funny money, and she went to Church's to spend it, not even knowing it was counterfeit."

"Damn, Key-man—that's messed up."

"Yeah, I know, right? But here's the kicker—some of that money she gave me last night? Six of the twenties were funny too."

"Oh shit."

"Yeah, doc, I know. And the crazy part? These motherfuckers damn near perfect. I would've missed 'em myself if I didn't know what to look for."

"Damn, Keith—maybe we need to hook up with that connect."

"Hell nah, B-Man—that's some fed shit. And my Black ass already on parole."

At 7:00, Keith hit Jonesboro Road. Before long, a few customers drifted through. An hour later, while he leaned on his car, talking on his cell, a smoke-gray Altima parked beside him. He hadn't asked what Angel drove, so he kept talking and kept eyes on the Altima.

A minute later, the driver door opened and a light-skinned, thick, five-foot firecracker stepped out. Small breasts, tiny feet, but everything else... white Guess shorts clinging like they might split. He guessed 25–30. He kept talking on the phone, measuring the sister with his eyes.

Angel decided to show off the bold side. She walked up, slid her arms around his waist, and very gently squeezed him—never taking her eyes off his.

"Uh—hold on a minute," Keith said into the phone, pulling it from his ear. "Excuse me—but I don't know you. You mind?"

"Well, Mr. Baylor, if you'd stop being rude, then not knowing me would be old news, and we could take care of other business."

"Other business? What the hell—oh, shit, my fault—hold up." He told the person on the line he'd call back—Renee's cousin had arrived.

Once he hung up, they got comfortable in Angel's car. Keith went straight to his pocket, pulling a roll of cash. Unfortunately for him, Angel had other plans—she cranked the ignition and pulled out.

"Hey—yo, don't go far, babygirl. I just need a minute to count your money."

Angel could tell he still didn't see the time it was—or he was trying to play faithful. Either way, time to kill the bullshit.

"Listen, Keith—let's get one thing straight. Personally, I could care less if you gave me a dime for my tramp-ass cousin. What I care about is what time it's gonna be with me and you. You feel me?"

"Me and you, lady? I don't even know what planet you came from—how in the hell you gonna hit me with that?"

"Because, baby—I am sick of hearing about you, Mr. Keith 'Good-Dick' Baylor, and then seeing you drop my little skit-ass cousin off so she can walk around acting like she's a diva. Now, I'm not gonna beat around the bush and play games. You want me to sign Renee's bond so she can get out? As payment—I want some fucking with!"

Chapter 33

Women love to act like only they get crazy, rude, or wild pickup lines. Truth is, a lot of men won't admit a woman can catch them off guard and knock them totally off balance. For a hustler, pride is everything and ego is armor. Angel's boldness clipped Keith right in the gut—but the instincts that make a man a man refused to fold. She was about to find out she was dealing with a grown-ass man.

"Angel—do me a favor and take me back to my car, please."

"Oh, so it's like that?" she snapped, attitude heavy, swinging into the Home Depot lot to turn around.

Keith took a few seconds, pulled a pack of Newports, lit one.

"Angel, maybe some broke-ass sucker would be happy to hear you offer him a piece of pussy. And honestly, another time that sucker might've been me. But unfortunately for you—I'm always on point. Make no mistake."

"Oh, is that right?"

"Yeah, babygirl—that's right. And do you mind explaining to me what you mean by 'on point'?"

She parked back at the BP by the 16 and stared.

"Listen, miss lady—if I decide to get sexual with any female, my reasons belong to me alone. Not because a fine-ass freak tried to back me in a corner."

"Excuse me—did you just call me a freak?" Angel said with a fake attitude.

Keith was already up on game and broke into laughter at the act. Angel laughed too—busted. For the next twenty minutes they sat in her car, trading jokes and talking. She ended up following him back to his job; they talked more for a couple hours about everything and nothing. When she finally dipped to post bond,

Keith gave her the money for Renee—plus an extra fifty on general principle.

He didn't know Angel was still a little heated about the sexual rejection. Life stays full of the unexpected, and Keith was about to experience something he wasn't prepared for.

At 1 a.m., he left work, headed back to Jonesboro Road on a paper-chasing mission.

***

"Man, Babyboy, I'm so fucked up over this bullshit—fuck!" Pain growled, barely holding it together.

"Look, cuz—calm down. We'll fix it."

"Fix it? Shit, B-Man—the motherfuckers stole my money, my dope, and my damn rims. Dammit, dog—all I got to my name is seventy-three dollars. What the fuck I'm gonna do with seventy-three fucking dollars?" Prin demanded through gritted teeth.

Babyboy knew his partner's anger wasn't at him, but the boiling rage made him uneasy. Someone had broken into Pain's basement and jacked his property—a major violation in their minds. Not once did Scott consider this the price for his own wrongs. All he could see was someone took what was his—and got away.

They sat on Babyboy's bucket, drinking Frïs vodka with grapefruit juice, trying to "put something together," not acknowledging that drinking slows the thinking. Nothing but freaks were coming their way, which only frustrated Pain more. The partners in crime decided to jump into traffic, see if any real opportunities popped. As they pulled off, Keith was rolling up, mind on making a few fast dollars.

***

"Q, boy, you a trip. If Keith was catching that much hell, he'd come to me."

"Ha! Rose, that's where most of you women mess up—you assume you know everything about your man," Nique said.

"Sweetheart, do you see Keith as the type to run to his woman with his problems?"

"Dammit, Nique—you make it sound like I'm calling my man a punk or something."

"No, hell, I'm not. That's just how your crazy ass took it. I was asking your opinion."

"Q, you gotta consider you know things about Keith neither me nor Roselyn do," Stacey said.

"That's an excuse—and you're beating around the bush," Nique shot back.

"Okay, okay, Mr. Smarty. No—Keith Baylor does not seem like the kind of man to tell his girl his troubles," Poochie admitted.

"And why you feel that way, baby—off observation only, nothing else."

"Well, Nique... to me, Keith is always in control. He just seems to always know the direction he's going."

"You see, Rose? Even Stacey doesn't see but the side of Keith he allows to be present."

"All right," Roselyn said. "Let's say I agree. You have to admit there isn't anything we can do to help the man without him asking."

"Yeah, yeah, Rose—I know. I was really just thinking out loud."

"No you weren't, Nique," Poochie laughed, punching him playfully. "You and Keith had this same conversation two days ago, and you wanted to talk to Rose then."

"Dammit, Poochie—you supposed to be on my side," Q said, grinning, caught.

The three friends were eating at The Rib Shack in East Point. Keith had been working hard and hustling harder the last three days—none of them had seen him. Q, who knew his best friend's habits better than anyone, felt in his gut something was wrong. He also understood that Keith—more big brother than buddy—

would never drag him into street business. So Nique was hoping maybe Rose could figure out what was troubling his main man—and then he could see how to help fix it.

Chapter 34

"Keith, this is some bullshit and you know it. If you weren't gonna get me out, you could've told me," Renee yelled into the phone.

"Renee—don't call me with no fuck shit. I gave your cousin that money on Saturday, so whatever your problem is, don't bring that to me."

"But Keith, my sister said you never came to her house."

"No, Renee, I didn't—because when I called, Angel told me she was the one signing the bond and she agreed to meet me on the block to pick up that bread."

"Bitch! Oh, that heffa is playing games," Renee snapped.

"Calm down. I'll have you out by tomorrow morning, I promise. But I want to ask you a few questions first."

"Okay, baby, what's up?"

"Tell me what type of chick Angel is. I mean it—because a couple hundred dollars ain't worth the trouble. This is just real stupid to me, you know?"

"Keith, baby, don't worry about the money. I'll make up for it as soon as I get out, okay?" Renee said, fear creeping into her voice. She suddenly wasn't sure he'd just "take care of it." The new edge in his tone told her he was too relaxed—and that made her fear for her cousin. Everybody who hung on the block knew what time it was with Keith's cousin Pain and his sidekick Babyboy. Nobody with common sense wanted drama with Scott "Pain" Baylor. Those thoughts ran circles in Renee's head so hard she almost missed what Keith said next.

"Renee, look—I'm off work today. I need to get off this phone and handle some things."

"Keith, be careful, please."

"Just be cool, and I'll have you out in a few more hours."

"Okay, baby—but let me call my sister and find out what's up before you go out of your way."

"A'ight, babygirl, do that. But no matter what, I'll make sure you're out by tomorrow. For real."

Keith hung up and hit the shower. He'd barely wrapped a towel around his waist when the doorbell rang. He didn't waste time looking for anything else to put on—just walked straight to answer the door, bare chest, towel knotted at his hips. Roselyn, Poochie, and Annette stood there.

"Shit—Roselyn, baby, you could've called first," Keith said, grinning as he hurried back to the bedroom.

"I'm sorry, baby. We were just up the street," Rose said, following him in.

"Well, good thing I at least had a towel on anyway," he joked, stepping into boxers.

Roselyn sat on the bed, watching him dress. Looking at her man was turning her on—reminding her just how damn good he looked.

"Uh-huh, Rose—try to remember you brought a little company with you," Keith teased, back turned as he searched for a shirt.

"Mr. Baylor, I don't have any idea what you're talking about."

"Yes, you do—you got quiet," he said, buttoning a polo. "Look, I got a few things to take care of. You and the girls can kick back and chill, but right now your man has to roll out."

"No, baby, we just dropped by because I wanted to check on you. But Keith—baby—is everything okay? I mean, I haven't seen you in almost four days, and when I do talk to you, you always 'in traffic.'"

The look on her face grabbed his full attention. For a minute he wasn't sure what to say. He sat beside her, took her right hand in his.

"Roselyn—what's on your mind, other than dropping by?"

"Baby, we haven't been able to see each other since we went skating because you're constantly on the go. Normally, we always find time. Now we're seeing each other less than average. That can only mean one of two things—and I refuse to acknowledge the first one. Which tells me something else is wrong."

Roselyn was smart enough not to mention her conversation with Nique, so she came at it from another angle. Keith wasn't the type to talk business—but he wasn't the type to lie to his woman either. He chose to tell her a little before leaving to make some more.

"Baby, things been a little rough for the home team the last few weeks. One of my business partners ran off with a lot of my money, and then one of my people got robbed. I'm on my way now to some paper so I can get Renee out of Clayton County jail."

Rose couldn't guess how much he'd lost, so she didn't know what to say. The first thing that popped out:

"Keith, baby—I don't know who this Renee person is, but please don't sign your name on anything, okay? If you have to pay that lady's bond, I understand. But please—have somebody else sign the paperwork."

Chapter 35

A natural human instinct is to protect what we consider ours. That feeling is strong in women—maybe that's why the Creator chose them to be mothers. Roselyn's first thought was to keep Keith safe. It wasn't that she didn't care about Renee; she didn't even know her. To Roselyn's way of thinking, that sister didn't truly exist. Keith Baylor was her man, and to Rose he was the only important factor. Period.

Riding in Babyboy's Buick with Pain, Keith thought about his talk with Rose earlier. The three men were on their way to Renee's sister's house to pay Angel a visit—12:30, Tuesday night. Babyboy pulled into the driveway. Two other cars were parked there besides Angel's Altima. Pain passed him a blunt. Keith sat in the back, smoking a Newport. He was about to open the door when the front door swung wide and out came Angel, Renee, and another woman he didn't know.

To say he was surprised wasn't close. The hard-knock hustler kept his composure, leaned back, dragged on his Newport.

"Yo, cuz—I see ol' girl went on and got your folks out," Pain said, lighting his own cigarette.

"Yeah, P—but I still wanna know what's what. You feel me?"

"Yeah, cuz—I hear you."

Renee and Angel walked up to the car; the other woman went back inside. Keith wasn't in the mood to meet-and-greet.

"Yeah, Angel—what part of the game you playing?" he asked, voice flat.

"Keith, baby, it's all right—" Renee tried, keeping her cool.

Keith shot her a look so cold and centered it shut her down. He turned back to Angel.

"I don't need a whole description from you. I already had your bullshit closer. So tell me—what kinda garbage you about to hit me with?"

"Listen, Keith—you don't have to call me names. I posted her bond—put my name and collateral up. Half my money's on the line," she snapped.

For a moment there was silence. Keith took another pull, flicked his cigarette, then spoke to Renee.

"Do me a favor."

"Okay, Keith—what you need?"

"Go back in the house and get your cousin's car keys. Pain will walk in with you and make sure she comes right back out. Matter of fact, both of y'all ride in the Altima back to the spot."

Angel didn't get a chance to finish whatever she was about to say—Keith was already easing out of Babyboy's Chevy. The women didn't get to rest either—Angel flinched when Keith's right hand gripped her jaw, firm enough to make his point.

"Now, listen. All I need is a reason—one more reason—to put you to sleep. Me, you, and Renee are gonna take a short ride. Cool with you?"

Angel bobbed her head in agreement. Renee hurried inside to grab the keys. Pain shadowed her to make sure she came right back. Soon both cars were off and in traffic—and what was about to go down wasn't what three of the four people expected. Only Keith knew.

"Keith, baby, I'm sorry I took so long, but I had important business to take care of," Angel said from the back seat next to him.

The whole time she tried to explain, Keith stared hard and said nothing. Not one word. The silence drove the thirty-something cousin nuts—and made Babyboy a little nervous, too. Truth be told, he was happy when he pulled into the Texaco and parked next to Keith's Camry.

Keith still didn't speak. He got out, leaving the back door open so Angel could get out, and waited between the two cars for Pain and Renee to join them.

"Say, Pain—I need to disappear for a minute. I'm gonna leave you the keys to my car. Meet me at my house at, say, five in the morning before you head home."

"Okay, cuz—that's cool," Prin nodded.

"Rose—you and Angel wait on me inside your cousin's car. I'll be ready to go in a few minutes," Keith said.

"All right, baby," Renee said, grabbing her cousin's hand and hustling back to the Altima.

Once the women were safely back inside—with Renee in the driver's seat—she started firing questions.

"Angel, girl, what did he say? Did he hit you? Curse you out? What happened?"

"Shit, Renee—he didn't say a fucking word. Creeped me the hell out. I thought I was gonna die. That crazy-ass man of yours had me nervous as hell."

"Hell, girl—you? When I saw those two crazy cousins of his, I damn near ran back in the house with Aunt Gail," Renee giggled.

Angel was about to say something else when the back door opened and Keith slid in with a leather backpack.

"Here—both of you, smoke this," he said, handing Renee a rolled blunt.

"Uh... Keith, Angel doesn't smoke weed, baby."

"Renee, did I ask you whether your cousin does or doesn't? Matter of fact, pass that to Angel and put some fire on it—now," Keith said, voice iron.

As they started smoking, Keith cracked the window so Pain could hand him two bottles of orange juice—each with a Platinum X pill floating inside. Pain passed them through. Keith gave one to Renee and the other to Angel.

"A'ight, cuz—have fun, dog. I got some shit to handle," Pain laughed, shaking Keith's hand.

"No doubt, cuz. I'll hit you in a few," Keith said, raising the window.

"Renee—that blunt gone?"

"No, baby, we just put it out for a minute."

"When you get on 285, make sure there's heat on that bitch—I want that burned before we hit downtown. Now start this ride up. We got a party to get to."

Chapter 36

Twenty minutes later, at 2:00 a.m., Renee was parking the Altima at the Atlanta International Hotel. Keith had already had SoBlack set up a suite the first night he came out, so the room was pre-planned—but the game plan had changed, and only Keith, Pain, and Babyboy knew how this night was supposed to go.

"Hey, Slim—Renee, go ahead and take a shower. Angel's up next when you come out," Keith said, pulling a .44-caliber revolver from his waist and setting it on a side table.

"Uh, baby... what's going on?" Renee asked, suddenly turned on and not sure why.

"Renee, shower. Angel—have a seat till she's done," he snapped.

Renee was quick. Angel slipped into the bathroom after her. The hot water sent tingles all over Angel's body and, by the time she came out wrapped in a white towel like her cousin, she was flushed and quiet. Renee lay on the king bed, watching Keith weigh up a quarter-pound of Green Gangster.

"Uh... Keith, me and Renee don't have a change of clothes," Angel offered.

Keith didn't answer at first. He stood, looked from Renee to Angel, then calmly undressed and sat back down—naked, eyes never leaving them. "There won't be a need for clothes for a little while anyway."

"Boy, put your clothes back on! What are you doing?" Renee blurted... while thinking, Damn, that man looks good.

"Calm down, Renee. Let's see if your cousin can be as bold now as she was when you were locked up," he said. "Angel?"

"Oh, it's like that, huh?" Angel smirked. "If you want to play..."

"Good. Game starts with you taking care of Renee before you get to me."

"What!" Renee yelped. "I'm strictly... y'all know I don't do no three-stuff!"

"Renee—drop the towel and close your eyes. Trust me," Keith told her.

Truth was, Renee was fronting. She was excited. Angel, a bona fide freak already warmed up, didn't waste time with more words. The energy in the room shifted, the lights went off, the TV flashed to an x-rated scene, and Keith slid onto the bed.

What followed wasn't tender or timid—it was grown. The weed and the "Platinum X" Keith had slipped into their orange juice smoothed the edges, and the three of them spent the night testing limits and erasing lines. By 5:00 a.m., they were spent. At 6:30, Keith woke to see the cousins tangled up again—and, of course, a player had to join the encore.

Chapter 37

SoBlack came to the suite to pick Keith up. Seeing the two women asleep in the bed hit her like a slap. She swallowed the heat, sat on the couch, and waited. Keith showered, dressed, and grabbed his bag.

"Y'all can call room service for breakfast or whatever. I'll be back through later, so chill or bounce—I'll leave that up to you," he said, walking out with SoBlack.

In the car, the silence was heavy.

"Blackgirl, I know you mad—you ain't said a word," Keith started. "Those two freaks don't mean shit to me. I did what I did because one of them tried to pull some slick shit a few days ago—came at a real one sideways. You feel me?"

"Keith, we not married. You don't owe me an explanation," she said, voice shaking. "What hurts is you didn't give me a damn warning. I came to pick you up and you rolling out the bed with two chicks. Two chicks in a room I rented for your Black ass. If you had a fantasy? Did it ever occur to you I might've been down with whatever you were down with?" Tears slid; she didn't wipe them. "Maybe I want to be something other than 'cool,' Mr. Baylor. Think about that."

The words rocked him. He spent a chunk of the morning thinking about SoBlack and looking at her in a different light. Pain was family, but this wasn't a cousin conversation—Keith had to sort it out himself.

Babyboy was knocked out on the sofa when Keith got home, so he forced himself to bed. He had to be at work at 5:30 p.m. Anyway. At 4:30 he woke to a quiet house—Pain must've left with Babyboy; his keys were on the kitchen counter.

He ate a quick bowl of cereal, caught himself spiraling over SoBlack again, then shook it off. "I'm not beating myself up all day," he muttered, dropped the bowl in the sink, and went to get ready.

Sometimes the most important things sit right in our face. If you're blessed or lucky, a good opportunity will circle back. But life in the fast lane doesn't always deal you the best odds—and you miss a lot of them chances.

"Rose, when you talked to Keith yesterday, did he tell you what was going on?" Poochie asked over the phone.

"Girl, we talked for a minute. I can't imagine the kind of money he's lost this past month," Roselyn said, merging onto I-75.

"Well, did you offer him some money or something to help out?"

"Hell no, Poochie! I'm not investing in no drug shit. Hell. No."

"Damn, Rose—that's your man, though."

"Yes, and I love him. But I work my ass off for my money—and I'm trying to save up to move into a new house."

Poochie knew about the house plan. She also believed a woman should stand with her man through good, bad, and ugly. The disappointing part was Roselyn had the money. It stung. Poochie looked up to Rose like a big sister—and now she wasn't sure how much of this to repeat to Nique, who was waiting to hear if Rose could figure out what was bothering his partner.

"Poochie? You there?"

"Yeah, girl. I'm here. Look—I'ma get off this phone. Call me when you leave from seeing Keith, okay?"

"All right, Poochie. Bye."

Chapter 38

"Sticky, baby, what did Roselyn say about Keith?" Nique asked as Poochie tried on a pair of sneakers in Foot Locker.

"Baby, she was on her way to see him when I talked to her an hour ago," Poochie said.

Not a lie, but not the whole truth either. She hated keeping anything from Nique—lately they'd been spending almost all their time together, talking about everything. That easy communication made their relationship glide. Still, that call with Rose had stirred up a few wild thoughts Poochie needed to get out.

"Baby... can I ask you something?"

"Yeah, Blackie. What's up?"

"This might sound stupid, but I want a real answer."

"Okay, Stacey. Something wrong?"

"No. I mean... yes—ugh. Nique, I'm tripping. Never mind."

"Calm down and talk to me. Whatever it is, it's all right," he said, voice soft.

She exhaled, slid off the shoe, waited until he sat back down beside her, eyes steady on her face.

"Nique... sometimes the people you think you know and the person they really are ain't the same."

"Okay, Stacey... and a dog has four legs. Now tell me what's bothering you—'cause you really starting to give me a hard-on," he joked, making her laugh—exactly what he wanted.

An employee drifted over. "Everything good?"

"Yeah, we straight," Nique said. "We'll take all three pairs, and maybe some matching shirts. Give us a sec?"

"Cool, just wave me down," the teen said and moved off.

"I think a lot of little girls would love having you for a father," Poochie said.

"'Cause I spoil my daughter rotten?" Nique grinned, resting a box on his lap. "Make no mistake, I ain't perfect—and I wouldn't be half as good without my mama guiding me. Now quit dodging. What's on your mind?"

"I'm wondering... would you have my back if I was on the verge of losing everything I have?"

The bluntness rocked him. He looked at her, let the question land, then answered clean.

"Stacey, listen to me carefully. I ain't the best person in the world, but I'm loyal to my people—sometimes to a fault. If you needed every dime I got, it's yours. Right now I only got about two grand sitting in the bank, but I can add another stack or two in a few days."

Warmth flooded her face. "Baby, I don't need your money. I just needed to know if I could depend on you like that."

"Oh—so you just wanted to check a big dog's pockets, huh?" he teased.

"Nah, boy—it ain't like that," she laughed.

"Good, 'cause I would've made you pay dearly for trying my gangster," he said, standing. "Matter fact, I got a better idea than shirts—how 'bout we take care of this situation in the bedroom, sis?"

Excited and more than ready, Poochie just stared back at her man. Nique didn't give her a chance to answer; he kissed her so hard it stole her breath.

"Wow," she whispered when she finally blinked back into focus.

"Oh, beautiful—that ain't even the beginning," Nique murmured, scooping up the boxes, taking her hand, and heading for the register.

“Uh—Nique, what about the T-shirts?” she stuttered.

“They’ll still be here when we find time to come back. Trust me.”

Chapter 39

At 8:10, Nique rolled up beside Keith's Camry and found his partner standing at the trunk talking with Roselyn. Poochie stayed in the car—on her cell with Nique's mom—which gave her an excuse to ignore her best friend for the moment. Rose noticed Stacey hadn't gotten out, but before she could address it, her own phone rang again.

"Yo, big dog—what's happening?" Nique said, nodding at Rose.

"Ain't nothing, Q. Same ole, same ole. Your Black ass ain't have to come all the way out here for house keys, fool. I coulda had Rose meet you when she left."

"Yeah, I know—but I got a bad case of the hot nuts, you know?"

Keith laughed, slid the house keys off the ring, and handed them over. "So you chilling on the S-O-B tonight, huh?"

"For now. My shit slow till later. Truth be told, I ain't in the mood to do much moving anyway."

"I can dig that, the way you been running. I ain't gon' keep you."

"Just ring me before you leave the house—I'll meet you somewhere."

"That's a bet."

They dapped and hugged. By the time Q pulled off, Rose was still on the line with Annette. She didn't get to confront Poochie—and figured her girl's wet-panties excuse for not hopping out would have to slide till later.

***

"Yo, Angel—where the hell is Renee?" Keith asked as he stepped into the hotel suite.

"She went home about ten minutes ago. We needed more clothes," Angel said from under the covers.

Keith wasn't trying to talk. He stripped while Angel watched. After the prior night with both cousins, she wasn't sure if she wanted a solo round—but last night's game had been her idea, and Keith wasn't here for mixed signals.

"C'mon, Angel. You pressed me when Renee was locked down. Now you got your chance," he said, climbing onto the bed.

There was no small talk. A brief kiss, hands positioning hips, a hard push into heat—then Angel caught her breath, braced, and met him. The tempo shifted; she took control, rolled it back on him until the room fell into quiet, television low in the background, both of them breathing hard. When she called his name, the moment snapped—Keith gritted through the edge and finished.

***

"Hey, Blackgirl—we need to talk," Keith said later, leaning against his car outside The Blazing Saddle. It was 4:30 a.m. SoBlack was dead tired and ready for a bed, not a conversation. But no matter what he did all day, their last talk kept replaying in his head. After the Angel detour, he was still frustrated—and done guessing.

"Keith, I'm tired. Can't we do this tomorrow?"

"Why—so tomorrow you can come up with a new excuse to duck it? Either we get this bullshit out the way now, or we can act like kids about it. I'm hoping we fix whatever's broken."

They stared at each other a long beat.

"All right, Mr. Baylor—let's talk. But I'm not standing out here. My feet hurt."

"Fair enough. Follow me back to my job—we can talk in private."

Chapter 40

"Today damn near drained the life outta me," Keith said, sliding his seat back as Tameka climbed in. "Can I enlighten you that it's Thursday morning now?" she shot back.

"Can I enlighten you that it's Thursday morning now," he parroted, earning a punch to the arm.

"Boy, stop playing. You said you needed to talk—so talk."

"I said we need to talk, but I won't press my luck." He exhaled. "I tried everything to stay busy and something happened to me that never happens—my thoughts kept coming back to you. Messed my whole day up."

He paused, then faced her fully.

"I guess I made the mistake of thinking 'cause you a dancer, you don't deserve to be treated like a nine-to-five woman."

"No," she said, steady. "You made the mistake of not considering I have feelings. That's what hurts."

"Guilty," he said. "We never really talked about 'em, Meka, so I'm confused how we even got here."

"We shouldn't have to talk circles about how we feel. Some things shouldn't need explaining. You don't come to my house to find another dude sitting there. I don't have you pull up and see me hugged up with anybody else. You ask me for anything big or small, I don't refuse. Maybe that's me being stupid."

"Nah—that's me not paying attention," Keith said. "But don't act like I could control how I feel. Dammit, Blackgirl, I care about you—but I'm in love with Roselyn!"

"I know, Keith. And that hurts," she fired back. "At least I don't have to worry about Rose being in my face. So she was never an option for me."

Silence snapped shut between them. For once, Keith Baylor had no words. He didn't want to hurt her; he knew he had. He also couldn't lie about where his heart sat.

"You're messing with my head," he said quietly.

"And you're messing with my heart," she said. "I can't make you love me. Let's just end the conversation, okay?"

"Damn, Tameka. I don't want us walking on eggshells when we're around each other. Tell me what you want, 'cause I'm confused as hell."

They held each other's gaze. Even a fool could see there were feelings on both sides; the question was what to do with them.

"You saying you're 'confused' sounds like an excuse," she said. "Do me a favor: think about Tameka when you get a chance. Maybe that'll help you out of it."

She opened the door, slid out, and drove away. The emptiness that settled over him was a different kind of hurt—one he'd remember.

—

"Girl, my stomach hurts like a mother—" Angel groaned, easing into a hot bath.

"Angel, it's Friday! You been walking around two days now whining. Hurry up if you wanna hit the club," Renee called from the toilet, shaving her legs.

Angel wasn't in the mood. For two days her body had felt off. The soreness wasn't fading; now she felt lazy and queasy in the mornings. Pregnant was the only thought that made sense. She didn't have kids, but she'd been down this road before.

"Damn. I need to talk to Keith," she thought, hearing Heather Headley humming softly from a radio in the hall.

"I'm not going to the club," she called out. "Go with the girls."

"What! Angel, come on now—you know good and well you the one driving," Renee yelled.

"You can drive. I'm sick."

"You really must be sick—'cause you hate people driving your car."

"And you must be forgettin' you were just driving it two days ago," Angel shot back.

"Yeah—and those circumstances were unusual."

"Look, you can use my damn car or stay home. Your choice. I'm not going."

Angel knew Renee would rush for the keys—folks without a car love driving somebody else's. As soon as her cousin pulled off, Angel called Keith and asked him to come by.

Chapter 41

"Hey, Keith. You busy?" Angel asked.

"Nah, I'm cool. What's happening, babygirl?"

"To be honest... can I see you tonight? I'd rather not do this over the phone."

"Okay. Give me twenty, twenty-five minutes. I need to check on something first."

"That's fine, baby. Bye."

"In a minute," he said, hanging up.

Traffic on the block had slowed; he could steal a short absence. It was 10:45 and he hadn't seen Pain or Babyboy—unusual on a Friday. He hit dial.

"Pain! Pain!"

"Run your mouth, cuz," Scott answered. "You hit me at a bad time—we on the move."

Warning bells. "Be careful, dog."

"I hear you. Holla in a minute, playboy," Pain said, clicking off.

Keith knew his cousin was out robbing somebody, and the bad feeling crept back in. He shoved it down, slid a Young Buck CD in, and turned the volume up. By the time he hit 285, "I Know You Gon' Let Me Shine" was rattling the Camry's speakers.

***

Angel opened the door in a Nike tracksuit—simple and clean, every curve outlined. No makeup, hair in a ponytail, toes polished fire-engine red. Keith caught himself staring.

"What's happening?" he asked, dropping onto the couch.

"Nothing much. You want something to drink?" Her voice had a nervous quiver.

"Yeah—what you got?"

"A little bit of everything. The Bud Light's cold."

"I'll take one of those."

"Damn," he muttered under his breath as she walked away.

"What did you say?" she called back.

"Nothing, shawty. Just wondering if I could smoke."

"Yeah. Let me get you an ashtray."

While she was in the kitchen, his phone buzzed.

"This is Keith."

"Hey, baby—you busy?" Roselyn asked.

"Not really. Just taking care of some small business. What's up?"

"I was gonna swing by your house after I leave Annette's. What time you getting home?"

"Right now, I'm not sure. Q and Poochie already there—you can head over."

Angel returned with the beer and ashtray, set them down, and sat beside him. He noticed she wasn't drinking. He checked the cap—still sealed. He lit a Newport, took a slow pull, a sip of beer, and waited.

"Okay, Miss Angel. Let's talk. Something's on your mind, or I wouldn't be here."

She inhaled, eyes on his, and just said it.

"Keith... I think I might be pregnant."

He didn't speak for a couple of long seconds. Shocked? Not exactly. Surprised? A little. If anything, he halfway expected those words to come from Roselyn, SoBlack, or even Renee—not Angel.

"Angel—it's only been, what, two or three days?"

"I know. But I know my body."

"Okay. Let's say you are. Then what?"

"Then I'd like you to be a good father. That's all I'm asking."

"What!" he blurted, sitting up. "Hold up, Angel—that's crazy."

"I'm not crazy. I've thought about this all day. I start my new job next week. I can afford a baby."

"Angel—what about Renee? Your cousin? You do remember her?"

"Yes, I remember who she is. Let me ask you a question—do you love my cousin?"

"Hell no. What kind of question is that?"

"The kind that matters in my situation. And since your answer is no, I'm sure about having my baby. All that's left is for you to decide if you want to be part of our child's life or not."

"But I'm not your man. I don't even see you like that."

"And I can be sure of one thing about Keith Baylor," she said evenly. "You'll do what's right by your child. No matter what we are."

There was no shifting her. Keith left with mixed feelings swirling. In the fast lane, one careless second can spin a whole new situation, outside your control. He was lucky in one respect—Angel wasn't looking for a free ride on his coattails. But like it almost always goes when you live fast, when it rains, it pours, and the road ahead gets hard to see.

Chapter 42

“Monica, appreciate you coming to get me.”

“Babyboy, where the hell is Scott?”

“Shit, Mone... we gotta talk about that while you drive. Just head to the block.”

“Hell naw, I’m not going anywhere till you tell me where the fuck Pain is!”

“Girl, calm down and pull off before the police roll up. I’ll tell you what’s what—just drive, okay? Fuck...”

Monica was slim, paper-bag brown, pretty like Meagan Good. She worked at Hartsfield and everybody on the block knew she and Pain messed around. Babyboy couldn’t think straight, so he hit the first name on his phone that made sense—Monica’s—and now they were on the expressway. His thoughts were sprinting a million miles a minute, replaying everything that led to him riding shotgun in her 4Runner.

***

Keith pulled into the 76, looking for a customer he’d arranged to meet. He parked at a pump and clocked Monica’s truck with Babygirl—one of Cap’s girls—posted at the driver window. He didn’t know what was up, but the tension in the air hit him as soon as he stepped out.

“Yo, Sticks—what’s the business?”

“It ain’t shit, Key-man. I need a dollar hard and a dollar soft.”

“I got you. Follow me to the trunk.”

While Keith handled Sticks, Babyboy came out the store and locked eyes with him. He froze, then jumped back in the 4Runner.

“Ride out,” he barked at a surprised Monica, who hadn’t spotted Keith yet.

"Boy—wait a minute. Babygirl and Cap need me to take them to their room."

"Tell them to come—before... you know what, never mind."

"Before what, Babyboy?"

"Nothing, Mone. Tell the bitch get in—now."

Monica pulled off. She saw Keith at his trunk with Sticks and almost stopped.

"KEEP GOING, MONICA! Fuck—man, keep going!"

"That was Keith at the pump. What's wrong with you? You know you gotta tell him what happened tonight."

"Yeah, yeah, Mone—I know what happened tonight," Cap and Babygirl said in unison from the back.

Babyboy cracked a Colt 45, took a long pull, and started talking—to a stunned audience that wasn't ready for what came next.

***

Around 1:15, Keith cut the ignition in his driveway. Roselyn's and Q's cars were still there. Inside the bedroom, his girl was knocked out in the middle of the bed, wearing one of his Lakers jerseys. A small smile crept across his face as he undressed. The hard-knock hustler was beyond ready for the land of dreams; at least there he could escape the world's tension and stress. He wrapped his arms around Rose and let go.

He didn't think about the fact that at some point he'd have to wake up—and sometimes what waits when you do makes you wish you hadn't.

Chapter 43

"Hold the fuck on, Angel! You're my damn cousin—don't come at me sideways like this," Renee screamed.

"Sideways? Bitch, please! Last I checked, me, you, and Keith were in that bed together."

"Ooooh—y'all was doing the nasty at the same time," Dee-Dee laughed, hand over her mouth.

"Dammit, Dee-Dee—it ain't funny!" Renee snapped.

"Listen, Renee—I'm not arguing all morning. Either you deal with it or you don't. That's on you."

"Oh, hell naw, Angel. Girl, you some bullshit. You wake up and tell me you think you might be pregnant by my man—and that's it, huh? 'Oh by the way...' Shit, Renee, you are so full of it I can't even believe you."

"You can scream, yell, whatever—but me and Keith talked last night, so... fuck it."

"Oh no you didn't, Angel! Bitch, you ain't been in here fucking my man while I've been gone—"

Renee rushed her. Dee-Dee grabbed Renee before it got ugly.

"Renee, you so stupid. Did I say anything about fucking Dex? I said I talked to Keith. Talked. That's all," Angel said, arms crossed, eyes hard.

Renee forced herself to breathe and calm down. She knew from experience she couldn't beat Angel straight up—her small cousin could handle herself. Pride had taken a major hit and there wasn't much she could do about the situation. That made it hurt worse.

"Can you at least tell me why?" Renee whispered. "Why do you want to have this baby?"

"If I told you the truth, you might not even understand—but I'll try." Angel exhaled. "When you and Keith left me in that room the other day, a lot ran through my mind. I thought about how hard it is to find the kind of man I'd want as my baby's daddy. While that was rolling around, I started looking at Keith that way and... it just felt right. So when I started feeling sick, I knew I'd keep Keith Baylor's baby."

Renee listened without a word. Tears ran down both their faces—a mix of too many emotions to name. Now it was time to try and rebuild however they could—both of them smart enough to know it would never be the same.

***

"Keith, your phone is ringing," Roselyn whispered in his ear.

"Baby, let it ring," he mumbled, pulling her closer.

"Boy, that phone been ringing non-stop for two hours."

"Then you answer it, Rose. I'm sleep."

"You so lazy," she laughed, then picked up. "Hello?"

"Hey—who this?"

"This is Roselyn. Can I help you?"

"Yeah, yeah—you can. You know where Keith at?"

"Yes. He's right here, sleeping."

"Oh, shit—my bad, shawty. Listen—when he wake up, tell him to call Silk at the barber shop. It's real important, you feel me?"

"All right, Mr. Silk. I'll tell him."

The phone kept ringing—one call after the next—until neither of them could sleep. At 12:45 in the afternoon he finally dragged out of bed for a shower. Q and Poochie had slipped out earlier; it was just Rose and Keith in the house. She came back into the bedroom with two glasses of orange juice and, as she sat down, both her cell and Keith's started ringing at the same time.

"Hello?" she answered, almost yelling. "Oh my God, Rae? Oh my God!"

"Hello? Ann, is that you?"

"Yeah, girl... Rose, have you heard from Keith yet?"

"Yes—Annette, I'm at his house now. He's in the shower. Girl—what's going on?" Chills ran up Roselyn's body.

Annette told her what she'd heard an hour ago—and why Keith's phone wouldn't stop.

Keith came out wrapped in a towel, answering his cell as he dried off. "This is Keith speaking. Run your mouth."

"Hey, baby—I'm so sorry," Renee cried.

"What's up, Renee? What the hell you talking about?"

Renee knew instantly he had no clue. She had to say what the whole block was buzzing about.

"Baby... oh, damn..."

"Renee, what the fuck is wrong with you?" he snapped, frustration rising.

"Keith, baby—I'm sorry, I'm so sorry—but I just heard that Pain was dead."

For a second he said nothing.

"Bitch, don't play with me," he exploded.

"But... but, Keith—everyone on the block is—"

"Bitch! Stupid ass bitch! I don't give a fuck what everybody on the block, corner, or town hall saying. Don't call me with that sucker shit unless you want me to stomp Jesus into your punk ass." He slammed the call closed.

The pure violence in Keith's voice made Roselyn's eyes bulge. She went silent on Annette's line. In her bones she knew Scott "Pain" Baylor was gone—and she thanked God she wasn't the one who'd said it out loud.

Chapter 44

"Rose, baby—I need to bounce. You can chill or do whatever," Keith said, pulling on a fitted Nike cap to match his tee and kicks.

"Okay, baby—just be careful. I'll take the spare key Nique left on the counter."

"That's cool."

She saw fear and worry in his eyes and had no idea what to say that wouldn't make it worse.

"Call me if you need me," she said, stopping him in the doorway.

"Yeah, baby. I will."

Minutes later, Lil Wayne's "Damn, I Miss My Dawgs" rumbled as he drove into a hard rain. No matter where you stood, you were gonna get wet.

***

"Yo, Keith, baby—what's crackin', player?" Silk shouted when he picked up.

"Say, Silky—turn your volume down a little."

"My bad, my bad. Doc, your girl tell you I called?"

"Yeah. I'll be in your face in a minute."

"Cool. Look—don't come in the shop. Pull up to the pay phone, I'll jump in and we'll turn a block."

"No doubt. One."

The block was jumping, and most of the crowd was there for one thing—the rumor Scott "Pain" Baylor was dead. Nobody knew for sure because Babyboy was missing, and folks were reacting to whatever Cap and Babygirl had started.

While Keith headed that way, his best friend was hearing it for the first time from Annette and Roselyn—and was rocked.

"Let me get this straight, Rose—Annette called while you and Keith were still here, and you didn't tell him?" Q asked.

"Look, Nique—he was already being told on the phone."

"What! And you let him out the damn house? Are you out your mind?" he roared.

For the first time in her life, Roselyn had nothing to say. Poochie knew her man was terrified for his best friend; the anger wasn't truly at Rose. Annette sat on the sofa quietly crying as Poochie rubbed Q's back.

"Fuck. Lemme see if I can get that fool on the phone before he snaps," Q said, pulling out his cell.

Before he could dial, it rang. He glanced at the caller ID and answered.

"Nique speaking."

"Yo, Q—what's the business?" Babyboy said.

"What's up, Babyboy."

"Shit, dog—nothing much. Laying low after last night."

"Oh yeah? And what happened last night, Babyboy? 'Cause somebody's gonna have to tell Keith how it just so happens his favorite cousin is supposed to be D.O.A."

Silence. Q heard him take a deep breath and let it out—maybe a hit of weed, maybe gathering his thoughts. More than likely both.

"Q—I ain't talked to Keith yet. Man... crazy shit happened. Me and C-L was out at Club Visions in Decatur looking for a lick. This cat sitting in his ride—some kinda something hooked up—so me and C-L made our move. Pain made the brother get out while I covered the lot with my chopper. Q, when cuz pulled off, I was right behind him in our whip. All of a sudden he starts swerving, and next thing I know the car up on the damn curb. I jump out, yank the door—Pain slumped over the wheel. I yell his name—he don't move. Q, I panicked. I hauled ass.

"I ain't even hear a shot, so I can't figure how he got hit. I done played that shit over and over in my head, dog—and I still can't tell you how he got fucked up."

Q said nothing, just let him talk. He hated being the one to pass this to Keith—but as soon as Babyboy hung up, he called his partner. Three women were sitting in front of him listening. Stacey, right beside him, heard Keith roar through the phone telling Q to get everyone out of his shit—and true to their friendship, Nique did exactly that. He knew his best friend. This wasn't a time to give the hard-knock hustler a crowd to crash into.

Chapter 45

"Yo, Slick—gotta roll to my folks' crib," Keith said as Silk opened the door.

"I know, dog. I understand, trust me," Silk replied, sliding out just as Q's call came through.

No one heard what the two friends said, but a few bystanders heard Keith roar, even if they couldn't make the words. An unfortunate crackhead, dumb enough to knock on Keith's window right then, caught the worst beating of his life in seconds.

"You stupid motherfucker! I told y'all never touch my shit!" Keith stomped and kicked the man. "I'm not to be fucked with today—period!"

He started to pull the iron from the small of his back.

"Keith! Keith, man—don't do it!" Lil C-Note and Silk yelled, grabbing him and wrestling him off the crumpled body. Angel—who had just heard from Renee—stood at the pump, tears running down her face. If not for Silk and C-Note, Keith Baylor would've picked up a fresh murder charge. They shoved him into his car. Silk slapped him once, hard.

"Player—make like dust and clear this spot before shit turns ugly. Get the fuck on. Now."

The slap snapped him back. He pulled off while C-Note and a barber dragged the crackhead toward the curb.

When he got home, he found a surprise: SoBlack sitting on his porch. Rose, Nique, Stacey, and Annette had left to give him space. At the same time Q was walking into the shop hearing what had happened.

"Hey there, Black—what's happening?" Keith said as they stood staring at each other.

"I'm sorry about Scott, baby. You want me to do anything for you?" Tameka asked, tears on her face.

"Nah—I'm cool. I kinda wanna be left alone, you know."

"Yeah, I understand. Let me get out your hair—"

"No... no, you good. Come on in. We can chill for a minute."

Keith cried in the shower like a five-year-old. He never heard the house phone ring—his boss calling for his number-one worker. SoBlack picked up, explained what was happening, and got him the night off. By the time he finished, the phone rang again—Babyboy, finally.

SoBlack was on the line with him, fixing Keith a strong drink in the kitchen. When Keith came out, she handed him both.

"Yeah—who this?" Keith said.

"Yo, dog—it's me," Babyboy answered.

"Oh, so you decided to call a brother. Ain't this a bitch."

"Keith, man—I've been fucked up about it all night."

"I'm sure. But B-Man—you shouldn't have left him. Dammit—you shouldn't have left him."

"I know, dog. I know, man—for real."

"No, Babyboy—you don't. 'Cause shit is all fucked up now—and nobody was prepared for this."

"I know, Keith. Please believe me, man. I know—and it hurts like a motherfucker," Babyboy cried.

It was hell for both men. Keith was angry—but he couldn't stay mad at Babyboy. Grief leaves no room for clean lines.

***

The next afternoon, Renee called: "Baby, where are you? It's twelve o'clock—the funeral's at one."

"Look—I'm at Charlie's Trading Post grabbing something to wear. Give me a minute," Keith said, holding up a pair of Dickies shorts to the clerk. He paid for three black Dickies short sets and a black fitted Dickies cap. Everyone riding with him to Pain's homegoing would be in black Dickies. Some of the street hustlers and family wore T-shirts with Pain's face on the front.

Keith, Renee, C-Note, and Silk rode in his Chrysler 300. Angel followed with her sister and two friends. Monica led another carload. Nobody said a word. At the church, they moved slow, signed the guest book, and took their seats.

Not everyone can see, feel, or walk in the shoes of a real street hustler—and hustlers come in levels. The robber lives different from the dealer; the con man different from them both. By chance or by path, they share at least one thing: sorrow and heartache. Each wants to be the best he can be in a hard world. How do they carry that weight and keep breathing? Only God knows.

After the service, they peeled off in different cars and slid back to the block. Keith called Roselyn to say he'd be at her house shortly. Silk and C-Note ducked into the shop. Monica, Renee, and Angel headed to Monica's apartment. And when the sun dropped, Tameka drove nowhere in particular while Keith sat quiet, wrung out. By ten he was out cold in SoBlack's bed—spiritually and emotionally beat.

Chapter 46

The days after the death of Scott "Pain" Baylor dragged at Keith's spirit, and for the first time in his life, the hard-knock hustler seriously thought about calling it quits on the street life. The family didn't have insurance on Scott, so everybody was pitching in to give him a proper send-off. Renee was in the hood hustling almost as hard as Keith, pushing her feelings about Angel to the side.

A warm summer breeze wrapped the thirty-two-year-old, light-brown-skinned hustler as he took a deep pull from a Newport. Around thirty people were still standing in the parking lot of Gus Thornhill's Funeral Home. Masking the storm inside with a calm face, Keith let friends pass without stopping him and locked eyes on a single soul in the crowd—his aunt.

He drew a breath for strength and walked over.

"Hello, Keith," Brenda Clayton said, smiling as she hugged her nephew. "Mr. Thornhill is waiting on you inside. He said they wouldn't close until you got here."

"Okay, Aunt Bren—thanks," Keith replied, hugging her back and flashing a quick, false smile before turning toward the doors.

He'd been late because Renee told him Monica wanted to come to the viewing but didn't know the directions. As Keith reached the entrance, Renee, Lil' Cee-Note, Silk, Annette, and Monica fell in step right behind him.

When he opened the door, he was greeted by Gus Thornhill himself—the former head of the East Point Police Department. The two men had a long history mostly built on Keith's law-breaking, but there was a layer of mutual respect that anybody could see as they talked a few minutes.

An attendant finally led them back to the casket of Keith's cousin, Scott "Pain" Baylor. Keith found himself staring down at someone in his life who could never be replaced—someone he'd forever miss. Anger, rage, frustration, and hurt flooded him. His chest tightened like the air had been sucked out his lungs. It felt like an asthma attack—he couldn't keep looking.

"Y'all be cool for a minute—I need a little air. I'll be right back," he said, and pushed himself outside, moving fast like he could outrun the pain.

He knew he had to share what he was feeling with someone—and only one person could hold it, no judgment, no belittling him while he was weak. He unclipped his phone and hit her number.

"Hello?"

"Hey there, beautiful," Keith said, a small smile tugging.

"Hey, baby. How's the wake?"

"Oh... everything is everything. Everyone's already gone. I was the last one to get here."

"Well, at least you made it. Tell me—are you alright?" Roselyn asked.

Keith let the question sit a beat. "Rose... you ever just need to know the answer to something—just because?"

"Yes, Keith, baby. I think everybody does."

"Rose, I stood in there looking at Pain and I felt like he wasn't supposed to be in that motherf— box."

As he said it, tears slid down his face. Roselyn could hear the heartbreak pouring out of her man, and one tear rolled down her own cheek as she listened. When he got himself back under control a little, she tried to lift him.

"Oh, so your bad ass ain't so tough tonight, huh?" she teased, smiling through it and dabbing her eyes.

Soon they were both laughing the kind of laugh only people who share something real can find in a moment like this.

"Baby, what are you going to do after you leave the funeral home?"

"Got a few people to drop off... then I don't know."

"Listen, whenever you finish—and I don't care what time it is—I want you to come out here. Okay?"

Keith didn't bother hunting for excuses. In his heart he wanted to be with Roselyn anyway. "Alright, baby. Let me go back in here for a minute, and I should be on my way in maybe an hour... hour-thirty."

Chapter 47

The funeral-home staff waited patiently when Keith and his group came back inside. His friends stood around the casket with sober faces. Everyone stepped aside as he approached, giving him space for one last moment.

Keith leaned over and kissed his cousin goodbye. No one expected it; no one knew how to react.

"This is it, cousin. I love you, boy. In a minute," he whispered.

They fell in behind him as he turned to leave. At the door, Keith stopped to sign the guest book, then they split into two cars and pulled out in silence, riding back toward the block. Keith called Roselyn to say he'd be at her house shortly. Silk and Cee-Note headed into the barbershop. Monica, Renee, and Angel left together for Monica's apartment.

Not everyone has the imagination to see, feel, or walk in a real street hustler's shoes—and hustlers come on so many levels. The robber's life and habits are nothing like the drug dealer's, and the con man is different from both. What they share—at least one thing—is sorrow and heartache, and a stubborn desire to be the best they can in a hard world. How they manage under all that pressure? Only God knows.

"Baby, where are you? It's twelve o'clock—the funeral is at one," Renee said on the phone.

"Look, I'm at Charles Trading Post grabbing me something to wear, so give me a minute, alright?" Keith said, holding up a pair of Dickies shorts and nodding to the clerk.

"Okay, baby—but everybody already started meeting over Monica's house."

"That's cool, Renee. All our folks know the drill. Tell 'em I'll be there in ten, fifteen tops."

He rang up three black Dickies short sets and a fitted Dickies cap to match. Everyone riding with or following Keith to Pain's funeral wore black Dickies. Some of the hustlers and a few ladies had T-shirts with Pain's face on the front.

Keith, Renee, Cee-Note, and Silk rode in his Chrysler 300. Angel had her sister and two more friends in her car. Little Monica followed with four dancers from The Blazing Saddle in her SUV. Cap came last with three of his chicks in a boxy '84 Fleetwood sitting pretty on chrome D's.

The service was already underway when the group of eighteen slid into the church, and their arrival turned plenty of heads. Truth be told, Keith didn't want to be around anyone; they took seats near the back. Twenty minutes later, they were on the way to the burial site, ready for final farewells.

As the casket lowered into the ground, tears ran down Keith's face. He drew a long breath, tore his eyes from the pine box, and looked around at every familiar face. Reaching for whatever strength he had left, he forced a grin and turned pain into a punchline.

"I'm not gon' keep standing here crying—my boy would've called me a sucker," he said, and the crowd laughed through the hurt. "Now I'm 'bout to go and burn the block down. If you drink or smoke, leave your bankroll—this one's on me."

For the next two hours the block held its own version of a farewell street party—jam-packed. Keith bought several bottles of Frïs vodka and Ruby Red grapefruit juice, with ice and red cups, serving them off his trunk. Atlanta PD rolled by during the gathering, but they didn't jump out or press anybody. It was beautiful—people embracing each other, drinking Scott Baylor's favorite mix, saying goodbye the only way they knew.

But there's always something that goes wrong...

Chapter 48

"Hey, Joe—Key-Man, book me, baby!" Crip, an old fiend from the hood, hollered.

"Say, Crip, doc—the bar is closed," Keith said.

"Damn, baby, don't do me like that. You still got a... what... bottle of that Super Ice left, my man?"

"No doubt, Crip—but this here is only going one way: mine." Keith shook the bottle in Crip's face, then softened. "Here—roll yourself a blunt on me. How 'bout that, huh?"

At the same time Keith was dealing with Crip, an unexpected crew rolled up. SoBlack, TyRo, Sultry, Passion, and Suede pulled in driving a money-green Navigator. Every head on the lot turned—their presence demanded it. Angel, usually comfortable in her own skin, suddenly felt aware of how she looked. Renee, on the other hand, was steaming as she watched the five women hug and kiss on Keith. Out of pure spite, she marched up and stood there until he acknowledged her.

"Yo, Renee—what's on your mind, baby?"

"Let me get the car keys, Keith. I'm about ready to go," Renee said, nasty on purpose to signal the dancers she was "with" Keith.

Bad move. Keith wasn't the type you tried to push—especially not after he'd already killed a half-gallon of vodka trying to bury his hurt. And now Renee came carrying herself like a child. SoBlack, TyRo, Sultry, Passion, and Suede traded looks of complete understanding.

"Bitch—since when you run my shit?" Keith roared. The parking lot went silent. Renee didn't say a word, and Keith kept tearing into her. "You see that's my point right here—folks always wanna play with the big dogs, but some of y'all can't think past go."

"Keith, baby, that's enough—you're hurting her feelings," SoBlack said, rubbing his arm, trying to calm him.

"Naw—hell naw, Black! My feelings been hurting me all motherfucking day, you feel me? And every time I turn around I'm looking at another ungrateful so-and-so. Hey, Renee—get your punk ass out my face before I permanently change yours!"

He shoved her away from his car, nearly knocking her over.

"Lil' Cee-Note—let's ride, pimp!" he shouted. "BlackGirl, follow me out to my crib."

That was all the excitement the block would get for the moment, because Mr. Baylor left the scene like smoke hit by air.

If Pain or Nique had been there when Keith reached the house, one of them—if not both—would've told him he was slipping, immediately. He walked straight into the kitchen, pulled a scale from a cereal box, weighed out the right amount of crack for Lil' Cee-Note, and headed back out.

Cee-Note was leaned in the Navigator's passenger window when Keith returned, chopping it up with TyRo, trying to get his mack on. Keith didn't interrupt—just slapped his young partner skin, passed him the 14 grams, and jogged back inside.

Coming out the bathroom, Keith nearly crashed into SoBlack.

"Damn, girl—you almost gave me a heart attack," he said, looking her up and down like the walking, curvy goddess she was.

"Boy, I just came to check on you before I take my brother's truck back. You okay?" Tameka asked, giving him a careful once-over.

"You could take care of one problem for me before you leave," Keith said, guiding her right hand against the semi-hard answer in his sweats.

This man had a serious hold on her heart—and he could short-circuit her common sense almost anytime. SoBlack caught herself biting her bottom lip, getting wet fast—then thought of her girls waiting outside. Before she could say no or "wait till later," Keith had pulled her into the bathroom and bent her over the sink, sliding her mini up over her cheeks.

It was raw, animal quick-love, and the couple enjoyed every single second of those ten minutes.

Chapter 49

When SoBlack hopped into the Navigator and backed out of Keith's driveway, Roselyn was pulling up with Poochie. Passion—sitting behind the driver—was first to comment.

"Hey, Black, looks like somebody's trying to get a little bit of your leftovers."

"Girl, what the hell you talking about?"

"Oh, bitch—don't play dumb," Suede chimed in. "We kinda already know your nasty ass just had a quickie. You all smiling and glowing."

"What gave me away?" SoBlack asked TyRo.

"Girl, when you came out damn near running to the car, Passion saw you digging out your panties," TyRo cackled, setting everybody off again.

It was a true all-girls moment. And Suede—the one who always said what she thought—couldn't help herself.

"BlackGirl, let me ask you a question, woman to woman. Me and TyRo were talking about the Baylor boys, and I been trying to figure out why you so in love with Keith's pretty ass. Dude got a twelve-inch or what?"

"Yeah, girl—or is his tongue game on paint?" Sultry jumped in.

For a minute, SoBlack was caught off guard. Then she got a little offended—until she glanced at TyRo and realized they were mostly playing. Tameka thought about Suede's question and picked her words.

"Suede, the length of Keith's thing is not y'all's business, and I'm not about to tell any of you how good, bad, or so-so his tongue game is—because that ain't your business either."

"Damn, girl—Fort Knox should give your Black ass a ward. The way you keep stuff private," Sultry clowned.

"See—that's why most females have trouble keeping their man to themselves," SoBlack said. "They tell everybody their business."

She took a breath. "If y'all must know why I'm in love with Mr. Keith Baylor, it's because he's different from ninety-five percent of the so-called men that try to run up on a sister. In Keith there's compassion, passion, loyalty, respect, determination, and honesty. He doesn't come at me with lies or deception, 'cause he never feels like he has to prove a point to anybody but himself."

"Damn, bitch—you need to marry his ass before he mess around and get away," Passion said. TyRo and Sultry nodded hard.

The conversation drifted to other things as SoBlack drove. It was one of those days girlfriends chose to hang out and find joy and comfort in a special thing called friendship. Tameka caught herself thinking about being Keith's wife, and the idea sent a storm of emotions through her chest. Refusing to let cement set around the thought of becoming Tameka Baylor, the tall, dark-skinned beauty hit the music and cranked it, R. Kelly's "Bump N' Grind" pouring from the speakers.

***

Roselyn was boiling after seeing the SUV full of women backing out of Keith's driveway. She completely ignored Lil' Cee-Note posted on the 300's fender, talking on his phone. Poochie knew her friend was about to start tripping—overreacting—so she didn't get out when Rose did. She sat in the passenger seat, slowly shaking her head, watching her best friend march into Keith's house.

Inside, Keith was lighting a cigarette and mixing a drink at the kitchen counter. No surprise crossed his face when he saw Roselyn—but if the hard-knock hustler thought this would be mild, he was in for a shock.

Instead of attacking straight away, the beautiful brown-skin sister tried an easy opener. "How was the funeral?"

"That's not the only question you want to ask," Keith said. "You brought tension through my door on your shoulders. However—answer to your first question: it was a funeral, Roselyn. I put my boy in a damn hole today. Now be careful with your next question, baby, 'cause you might not like the answer."

His bluntness shook her, but she pushed past it.

"Oh, we feeling cocky today? I came by to check on you 'cause I knew the funeral was today—and I pull up to find your driveway full of bitches!"

Keith stared at her like he was seeing a different Roselyn for the first time.

"Keith, I don't know what your problem is, but I need you to tell me what's up."

"What's up with what, Roselyn?"

"Don't play stupid, Keith! You know damn well what I'm talking about!"

Silence stretched while he measured her with his eyes, testing how much truth she could really handle. The vodka had him harder than he thought. In his mind, he was sober.

"It's a trip how you can come at me about my business, but I never press you about a damn thing," he said, voice rising.

Chapter 50

"People like you kill me—trying to stress a man," Keith snapped. "You never got females confronting you about me. You never once caught me doing foul shit with a chick—but now you come up in my pad questioning me about what? Nothing. Nothing whatsoever, Roselyn.

"I'm a street dude, Rose. I don't got a nine-to-five at Coke-Cola, IBM, or Georgia Power. I get up seven days a week and hustle my black ass off just to have a little bit of life's nice shit. Do you even understand that?"

The volume made Roselyn jump. She'd never seen him like this—and she knew better than to push him further.

"Keith... how much have you had to drink?" she tried, hoping it would drain some anger.

Wrong move.

"What kind of question is that, Rose? You trying to imply I can't handle my liquor, huh? I tell you what—get the fuck out."

"What? Keith—wait a minute. What do you mean?"

"You heard me, Roselyn. Get the fuck out of my spot."

She didn't waste a second asking anything else; she bolted like the Hulk was after her. Minutes later, Roselyn and Poochie were gone, and Keith slumped in the 300 with Lil' Cee-Note and peeled off toward the block.

***

"Renee, you know good and damn well you picked the wrong place and time to start some shit as usual," Dee-Dee said.

"Fuck you, Dee-Dee. It's none of y'all business what goes on with me and my man anyway."

"Huh—whatever. Your man? Please. Funny how Keith is 'your man,' but your cousin Angel the one carrying his baby," Monica said, glancing at Angel, who hadn't said a word.

"Whatever—and I got your bitch too," Renee shot back.

None of them really wanted drama. Most of it was just talk—everybody was raw and emotional. By the time Keith pulled into the No-Gas Station at 8:30, almost everybody had left.

Sidney J. Percy—better known as J.P.—was at the register trying to get with Felicia the cashier. J.P. and Keith were former partners in More Hustle, Inc. Keith, for the most part, was the money man; J.P. the mastermind behind the bootlegging program. They'd gotten cool doing time together and kept in touch after. Everything had been smooth—until J.P. ripped him off. J.P. was so busy laying his Mack that he didn't see trouble walking through the door.

"So tell me, Lee-Lee—we getting together tonight or what?" J.P. asked.

"I don't know—maybe. Let me think about it, okay?" Felicia smiled.

Keith walked in and completely missed J.P. because he was answering his ringing cell. Angel had moved to the passenger side of her car, away from Dee-Dee, Renee, and Monica, so she could call him.

"What's up, baby girl—run your mouth," the hustler said.

"Hey, boy—I was just calling to tell you me and my sister are about to leave."

"I can dig it, Angel, 'cause I'ma be around on the block for a minute."

"Oh—okay. I guess I'll talk to you later then," Angel said, feeling extra emotional behind the pregnancy.

Keith had really started to like the cool, light-skinned sister, and he knew she just wanted to kick it. "Come inside the store," he told her.

Walking back from the cooler with a can of Bull, Keith grabbed a big bag of plain potato chips. As he turned from the racks, he caught a glimpse of J.P. in the overhead mirror. First he thought he was seeing things—but when he rounded the aisle and J.P. laughed, Keith got a better look.

Already under the influence with a second rag of vodka settling in, the hard-knock hustler went hot.

"Son of a—" was all that made it out before Keith rushed J.P.

Some alarm went off in J.P.'s head because he turned just as—

"BOOP!"

"Agh—oh, shit!" J.P. cried, catching the can of Bull in the face. Keith had aimed for the back of his head.

"Yeah, you bitch-made punk—I got your ass now!" Keith yelled, punting him in the private collection.

"Ahhh—oh—shittt!" J.P. folded to his side.

"Don't ball up now, nig—! You wasn't balled up when you was stealing my shit, hurt? Did you?" Keith roared, stomping down on J.P.'s left hand. The dark-skinned brother screamed, ear-splitting.

Angel stood there shaking as she watched Keith go crazy. Out the corner of her eye she saw the manager snatch up the store phone—police would be rolling soon. She ran up on Keith, crying his name as loud as she could. At first he didn't hear her; out of pure reaction he threw a nasty right that would've clipped anyone his height.

It sailed clean over Angel's head. She screamed and wrapped her arms around his waist. Hearing her crying broke through. He eased her off.

"I'm cool, Angel. Let me go, okay?"

"Keith—the police are coming."

"I know—so let me bounce, outta here." He wasn't about to leave without grabbing some of his money back. J.P. tried to fight him off as the hard-knock hustler dug his pockets—but that only made Keith dig faster.

Chapter 51

Word spread fast through the lot about what went down inside the gas station, so nobody was surprised when two Atlanta PD cars flew onto the scene. Keith had vanished from the T6 only minutes before they arrived. Angel, Renee, Dee-Dee, and Monica were just managing to pull out as the cops were rolling in.

As usual, nobody left behind was "cooperating." J.P., soon loaded into an ambulance, played too-hurt-to-answer, milking it. Babyboy, sitting low in a Camaro across the street, dialed Q and gave him the quick version.

"You mean to tell me Keith just stomped some dude, but you don't even know why?"

"Look, Q, I'm in a damn crackhead's ride—you already know the deal."

"Yeah, yeah, I know what time it is. Wish you could at least tell me what the cat looks like."

"When I find out more, I'll hit you with the spill. Right now—I'm ghost," Babyboy said, hanging up.

Pulling away from the block, he couldn't help thinking how things in the hood never stay the same. Shaking his head, the young robber/dealer knew one thing: Keith Baylor was not the person to piss off right now.

***

"Renee, girl—wasn't that Babyboy in the pawn shop lot?" Monica asked, checking her rearview.

"I don't know, Mone—I was looking the other way."

"Girl, I know your ass was trying to clock which way Angel's car went," Monica laughed.

"Monica, ain't a damn thing funny. I should be the one having Keith's baby—not my damn cousin. Damn, this is some bull."

Monica glanced over as they rolled down Jonesboro Road. The hurt on Renee's face wasn't for show.

"Renee, I gotta ask you something for real. Are you hurt because Angel is pregnant—or because it's not you?"

Renee whipped her head so hard Monica swerved a little. "Mone, I might not be having such a hard time accepting it if it wasn't for the fact I'm in love with Keith."

"Hah—now that's a thought, Renee. I ain't never known you to have 'feelings' for any of these dudes out here."

"Yeah, well... shit happens. And the fucked up part? I never even wanted kids."

"Wow. That's deep."

"You know what I'm saying? Trust me, I know. I just realized I'd do anything for Keith—even have the motherfucker's children," Renee blurted, leaning her head back against the rest.

"Well, girl, there's only two things you can do. Stop messing around with Keith and let Angel have him... or keep dealing with him regardless, 'cause there really ain't shit else."

Nothing left to say. Renee sank into her thoughts—everything Keith Baylor.

***

Keith slid into Washington Circle Apartments in East Point, just driving with no destination. The projects were alive—people everywhere. He looped the block, spotted a space, and parked. Faces he knew clocked the brown-skin brother in the pretty car.

Skip, Ronnie, Moon, and Milkman were perched on a set of steps, watching as he walked up.

"I'll be damned—must be about to snow," Skip joked.

"Damn sure is. I need to run and get my coat," Milkman added, both standing to dap and hug him first.

“Moon, Ronnie—what’s up?” Keith nodded, leaning his back to the rail.

“Damn, my guy—what brings you to our neck of the woods?” Milkman asked, sipping his 40 of Colt 45.

“Shit, Milk—I was just out riding, swung through. I can see the crowd still the same out here.”

“Yeah, well—the whores still whoring and the smokers still smoking,” Moon chimed, cracking everybody up.

“Hey, Keith—you know your girl Pumpkin got an apartment now, down on the end,” Ronnie said, sparking a cigarette.

“Oh, hell naw, Ron—don’t start no shit. You know damn well I ain’t messing with your powder-head cousin,” Keith shot back, the steps crew howling again.

East Point PD rolled by, gave them a hard look, kept it moving. Around 11:30 the girls finally found the nerve to approach; by midnight everyone drifted their separate ways. Keith ended up at the IHOP in old Hapeville with a thick, heavy-rear sister everybody called PorkChop, face like Serena Williams. At 2 a.m. he took the 30-year-old bow-leg home and sat in her car chilling for another hour.

He half wanted to bring her to his house—but he wasn’t in the mind for sex. He just wanted to relax with cool company and talk about nothing. PorkChop was perfect for that. He was so caught up he ignored his cell—call after call. One was Lil’ Cee-Note, trying to re-up, but tonight Key-Man was mostly MIA.

At 3:10, on the way home, he finally answered when ANGEL flashed on the screen.

“Yo—what’s up, baby girl?”

“Oh, nothing really. Couldn’t sleep, so I called to see if you were alright.”

“Oh, so you were concerned about a brother, huh?”

"Yeah—you know I had to check on my baby daddy," Angel laughed.

"I can dig that. Listen—throw something on, I'll swing by and scoop you."

"Okay—how long?"

"Ten minutes maybe. But I ain't trying to see your cousin."

"Oh—Renee spent the night at Monica's. She isn't here."

"Cool, Angel. I'll be there in a minute."

He picked her up and took her to his place, handed her a Lakers jersey to sleep in. Soon they were both out. Slowly, their relationship was changing—and not because either was forcing it. As Keith drifted off, it hit him: he'd gained a baby mother—and, above all else, a friend.

Chapter 52

"Man, Keith—man! I tried to get at you last night so I could get back on," Lil' Cee-Note said into his cell.

"I got your message, Cee-Dog—it was there when I woke up. What time you coming out?"

"Shit—Cee-Note, boy, I just got out the shower. Give me a minute."

"That's cool, Key-Man. Just hit me—I might not be at the barber shop."

"I got you, Cee-Man. One."

It was a quarter to three and Keith hadn't done much yet. He and Angel had gone two rounds since waking up, then she helped him in the kitchen and the two of them ate. Now Angel was sleeping like a kid with her head on his stomach while he scrolled through the missed calls—PorkChop, SoBlack, Roselyn, Renee. Business first, though.

***

"Rose, you still haven't heard from Keith yet?" Annette asked.

"Hell no. I called his ass before we left for church. When you drop me at home, I'm going by the block. More than likely he'll be at the shop trying to make some of his money back."

"I understand. They spent a gang on Pain's funeral."

"Shit, Ann—Keith came out his pockets so much you'd think he rich—but I know damn better," Roselyn said, feeling guilty about yesterday's blow-up.

"Well, girl, it's 4:30 now. You sure you don't wanna ride down Jonesboro Road now?"

"Naw. Me and Keith need a serious talk, and I won't ask you to wait up. Just take me home so I can put on something else."

Roselyn, Annette, and Poochie didn't know about Keith's run-in with J.P. the night before. Poochie was hearing about it right then—because she was at the park picnicking with Nique.

***

Poochie lay on a blanket beside Q, reading a Tami Hoag novel. Q's head was on her thigh, thoughts a million miles away. She turned a page, saw that look on his face, and caught his eyes.

"Nique, we're supposed to be here relaxing. Mind telling me what's running through that head? And don't lie—your little veins show up in the middle of your forehead."

"Damn—I'm busted," Q laughed. "Stacey, baby—I'm just worried a little about Keith. That's all, for real."

"Nique, Keith is a big boy. He can take care of himself."

"I know—like he 'took care' of Sidney yesterday. Huh—Sidney."

"Nique... who is Sidney?" she asked, concern rising.

"Shit—my bad, baby. Up here—Sidney was in the joint with me and Keith. I never really cared for dude, but he was cool with Keith, you know? Anyway, J.P. and Keith got into that bootlegging business together—More Hustle, Inc. Keith, at first, was the money man. As time moved on, he gave J.P. more responsibility. I told Keith I didn't trust that motherfucker, but Keith is the type to trust you till you give him a reason not to.

"Not long ago, J.P. stole everything from the shop—movies, CDs, cash—everything—and disappeared. I told Keith, Stace. I told him I didn't trust that bitch. But Keith was back in the drug business with both feet—'cause of Pain's crazy ass. I'm telling you, these last two months been so fucked up. And now Keith caught J.P. slipping on the block—damn near broad day."

"Where did this happen, Nique?" she almost yelled.

"Heat Cash Station—yesterday, far as I understand."

"Damn—Rose is gonna have a fit."

"No, she not, Stacey—'cause it ain't Roselyn's business."

"But, baby—Rose should—"

"No. No—Stace, no. It is not my or her business. Period. Leave it alone," Q said, firm.

Silence—heavy but needed. Poochie sipped wine while Q queued up Frankie Beverly & Maze, Live in New Orleans. The couple settled back into a beautiful evening together, pushing the "Keith situation" to the back burner—for now.

Chapter 53

The dice game on the side of the T6 station was in full swing when Keith pulled up. As soon as he popped the passenger lock, Lil' Cee-Note handed him $380.

"Key-man, I owe you twenty more. Gimme a few minutes and I got you," Cee-Note said while Keith counted.

"Lil' Cee, knowing you, your young ass is over there gambling—but it's cool. If all I had to wait on every day was twenty funky bucks, I could stop smoking. Go on and do your thing. I'm finna run in the barbershop and let Silk line me up. Hit me when you ready."

After the cut, Keith slid into a seat in front of Old Man Renard and set up a chessboard. Business kept tapping him on the shoulder—seemed like everybody wanted to smoke tonight—so every fifteen minutes he stepped outside to serve someone and came back to Renard's pawns creeping.

A little after five, Roselyn walked into the shop. Keith's eyes lit like a lamp. She took a seat, crossed her legs like the queen she was to him—silk summer dress, thin straps, chunky wooden sandals—and his mouth went dry. That hungry look in his eyes made Roselyn warm all over.

Keith couldn't focus on the board anymore. He pulled his phone. "Cee-man, I'm 'bout to slide. Meet me at my 300," he said, already standing.

"Damn," was all he managed before he and Roselyn met halfway and kissed—slow, deep, nothing polite about it. When they finally came up for air, foreheads pressed together, Old Man Renard broke the spell.

“Damn, boy, get a room!” he barked, popping the shop and drawing laughter.

“You know I’m all messed up behind you, right?” Keith murmured.

“I know, right,” Roselyn giggled.

“Dammit, Keith,” Renard called, “with all that money, take that pretty girl somewhere decent. If she was my daughter I’d crack you upside your head!”

“More than likely, you just wish you were thirty-five again,” somebody joked, and the whole shop laughed with the customers.

“Okay, Mr. Renard, you right. Y’all be cool,” Keith said, still holding Roselyn’s hand as they slipped out.

***

Later, Roselyn lay on the bed—bare, open, vulnerable—and Keith kissed a path up her body. Their chemistry was unreal; even talking felt charged when they were together. Roselyn was confident in her skin, and Keith was the first man who could pull the rawest desire out of her without a word. She drew him close; he answered with all that slow, deliberate pressure she craved. The rhythm built, the room vanished, and they lost themselves in each other until the only sound left was ragged breathing in the dark.

Attraction has its own power. Two people can be perfect in the sheets and strangers outside them. One of life’s cruelest truths is being in love while your partner is only in lust. One heart can’t love hard enough for two—unless someone in that relationship is a fool.

Chapter 54

"KISS 104.1... brand-new from the beautiful, talented Leona Lewis—'I'm You.' Kick back, grab that special someone, and enjoy Atlanta's best... Hot KISS 104."

Leona's voice poured through the 300 as Keith pulled away from Roselyn's place. Loving her always left him wanting more, and if he didn't force himself to get out of that bed, he knew they'd overdose on each other. He grinned at the thought—then the lyrics caught him:

So you think I'm strong, but you're acting weak...

But baby, I'm you...

Chills ran down his arms. By the time the song faded he was talking to himself. "Boy, get your head right, Mister Baylor." He dug for a Newport. "Damn, when did this happen?" he muttered.

Then Guy's "Let's Chill" came on, like the radio was clowning him.

Across town, Angel walked in to find Renee counting out tiny baggies in her room. Normally she'd knock and keep it moving out of respect, but tonight her nerves were raw. One look at Renee's face told Angel her cousin was up to no good—and the dope was Keith's. Angel bit back a dozen sharp words. Sometimes the heart outruns the mind we're supposed to think with.

She stepped into the hallway, opened her purse, and dialed Keith. Voicemail.

Stress can be treated like trash: if you don't want either, don't leave a message. Real talk. BEEP.

A few seconds of Anthony Hamilton's "Charlene" played before the tone. Hearing it made her feel worse; everyone knew how deep Keith was into Hamilton's music. No use leaving a message; if he was free he'd pick up. She hung up and exhaled.

***

Keith made a decision: once he moved what he had left—both on the streets and in his possession—he was retiring from the nonsense. Merging onto I-285, his phone buzzed again.

"Yo, Q, run your mouth," he answered.

"What's up, big bro," Nique said.

"Ain't shit, baby—out and about, you know me."

"Hold that thought. Other line," Keith said, clicking over. "Hey, Porkchop."

"Hey, baby. You working?"

"Yeah, doll, I'm on the clock. What's on your mind?"

"A few folks over here looking for something."

"I can dig it—but what team they trying to join?"

"They play softball, but one or two thinking about the Green Gangsters," she laughed.

"Tell your peeps give me fifteen. I'll be in your face," Keith said, then clicked back. "Q—you still there?"

"Yeah."

"Bet. You trying to do the buy-in tonight?"

"Yup. Hit me when you in route so I can meet you there."

"Say less," Keith said, and they hung up.

Sometimes ignoring your first mind gets expensive. Things look smooth, we relax, and distraction creeps in. If we're lucky—or blessed—we get a warning.

Keith slid into Washington Circle. Business with Porkchop went smooth—both the work and the conversation. On the way out he clocked East Point PD rolling slow, making their presence known. He lit a cigarette and took his time walking to the car. When the cruisers slipped out of sight, he hopped in and burned rubber out of East Point.

At 3:30 a.m., talking to Porkchop as he turned into his driveway, he was greeted by Soblack waiting on the porch.

Chapter 55

"Keith, baby, I'll take care of the lights, gas, and water after I hit the bank. Anything else you need before I start running?" Soblack asked, tucking the cash and bill stubs he'd handed her into her bag.

"Yeah—the cell bill. But I'll handle it if you got other things," he said from the doorway.

She pulled off. His phone rang before the taillights cleared the street. "Private" scrolled across the screen; then a second call cut in—Lil' Cee-Note.

"Run your mouth," Keith answered.

"Key-man, I need to get straight. I'll be in traffic in a few."

"Meet me at the pawn shop," Keith said. "We need to turn a block first."

"Cool. One."

Jonesboro Road was bumper-to-bumper. It took fifteen minutes just to swing into the old pawn-shop lot. Inside, Keith scooped what he needed; outside, he passed Crip a few dollars to hold him over.

"Yo, Crip—I'ma fuck with you later, my guy."

"I can dig it, Key-man, Laker," Crip said, limping off.

"Come on, Cee—we need to roll," Keith said, heading for the 300 with Lil' Cee-Note on his heels.

"Hey, Keith! Say, Keith!" Kathy Wilkins—lean, golden-brown Mexican shorty, a legendary trick-turner from one end of Jonesboro to the other—flagged him down.

“What’s up, Cat-baby?” Keith said, driver door open, one leg still out.

“Hey, baby, I need to get right. Today.”

“Shit, Cat, I’m on my way to make a move now. All I got left is a funky fifty, but you can get that on your face card.”

“Damn, boy—you a sweet ass nigga. That’s why I fuck with you,” Kathy said, kissing his cheek as she palmed the bag. She licked her tongue at him with a wink and headed off.

Keith wasn’t worried; her word was platinum among the regulars.

He eased onto I-285. In the rearview, a dark-green Ford tucked in two cars back. Unmarked. No question.

“Yo, Lil’ Cee—you ain’t done nothing dumb, have you?” Keith asked, still watching the mirror.

“Nah, Key-man. Why you ask?”

“’Cause there’s an undercover behind us, that’s why.”

“Man, I just got on the block. I ain’t got jack but some dro. You got license and all that, don’t you?”

“Cee-Note, don’t ask me no dumb shit. You know I keep it straight,” Keith said, fishing for a Newport.

Before the lighter sparked, the green Ford slid up alongside the 300. Next thing he knew, three plain-clothes cops were swarming, guns out, voices cracking the air.

“Put the car in park and get the fuck out!”

“Shut the car off and get the fuck out!”

A Black undercover leveled his pistol toward Keith's face. "Hands where I can see 'em! Now!"

Chapter 56

The passenger door ripped open—Lil' Cee-Note yanked out by a white undercover in black fatigues stamped ATLANTA POLICE across the chest. Keith got dragged from the driver's seat and shoved into the waiting arms of another plain-clothes cop. The first officer with the gun slid behind the wheel of Keith's 300 while the other two stuffed Keith and Lil' Cee into the back of an unmarked.

No explanations. No rights read. They pulled off Jonesboro Road and parked behind a white police van in the Home Depot lot, tucked from public view. An hour crawled by before the Black undercover from the traffic stop strolled up to Keith.

"You got a driver's license?" he asked.

"Of course I got a damn license. What's this about?"

"About you being in possession of cocaine."

"Man, you full of shit. I don't got no hard! I ain't touched that," Keith snapped.

"Uh-huh. Where your registration and insurance?"

"In my car. Center console."

A couple minutes later the cop came back cheesing like a five-year-old on Christmas. "You on parole or probation, Baylor?"

"If I am, what that got to do with anything?" Keith shot back.

"Because then you'd be a convicted felon... which would make your charges several. Like—possession of a firearm by a convicted felon."

"Bullshit," Keith growled.

"Tell you what—if your sidekick claims the weapon, we'll think on letting you go. Otherwise, you know how this goes."

By nightfall Keith was shackled in a paddy wagon with seven more bodies—including Lil' Cee-Note—charged with:

- Possession of a firearm by a convicted felon, and
- Possession of marijuana with intent to distribute.

The cops took everything: Keith's cash, his cell, even the car—impounded. Being on parole made the mix extra deadly. This was a storm he wouldn't forget.

"Pre-trial—what's the status on Mister Baylor?" the judge asked the next afternoon.

"Ah—Your Honor, his status falls in the S.O.B. category," the solicitor said.

"Excuse me, Your Honor," Keith cut in. "Can I speak with my attorney one second, please?"

"All right, son. Make it quick."

Keith pulled his public defender aside. "Listen, I don't want no S.O.B. bond—ask for a regular bail amount."

"You sure?" she whispered.

"Yes, ma'am. I'm sure."

Keith had sat in Fulton County before; a signature bond would just sit while parole flagged him. He needed a real number, real fast, or he'd catch a hold and rot. Calling Roselyn on the day-room phone cost him pride and patience.

"Baby, why it take you so long to call me?" she asked, breathless.

"Rose, I only got a minute. I need you to come bail me out—like now."

"Okay, but I gotta reach my brother before I call his bondsman. Give me a minute. Are you okay?"

"No. I'm not. If I'm still in when my P.O. finds out, I might as well not have a bond, you feel me?"

"Okay. Okay, baby. I got you covered."

Roselyn hung up and looped in Soblack for Keith's lawyer info. She tried everything, but the locks didn't spring that night. Next morning, Keith lay on a steel slab teaching himself not to hope... until his name blasted out the loudspeaker.

"BAYLOR! Pack it up—all the way!"

He smiled despite himself. Roselyn must've worked magic. A C.O. popped the door. Keith scooped his property, signed the paper, and followed the escort toward daylight.

Chapter 57

When he glanced through the glass of the exit door, the sight hit him in the chest—Soblack waiting, hands folded tight, eyes wet. For a second time slowed, and all he could see was the hurt he'd put on the people who loved him.

Later, at home, Keith started dialing. "What you mean you ain't seen Renee?" he barked into the phone at Angel.

"She left out the blue and nobody knows where she went. I tried to call you four days ago, but you didn't answer—what you want me to do, Keith?"

"Not a damn thing. That's what you always do—nothing." He slammed the phone down, rage ricocheting off the walls.

Everything was wobbling: cousin dead, Renee missing, the block hot, parole breathing, and now this arrest. Soblack had taken off work and run papers all day just to pry open the door for him. They were both emotionally and physically cooked.

At some point the noise inside him got too loud. Keith slid to his knees on the bedroom carpet and poured it out.

"Father in Heaven, I know I'm a disappointment to You. I'm a disappointment to myself. I'm a hustler, a thug, a dope dealer—and I need Your help. I'm not gonna run a thousand lies. I gotta talk before I lose my mind and do something stupid. My life is a mess and I don't know how to fix it. I need You more than I ever did. Please... have mercy on me."

He prayed until his body ached. When he finally crawled into bed, sleep found him like rain.

He woke with a mouth like sand. After two glasses of water he reached for the phone and called Roselyn.

"I'm home," he said.

She exhaled a smile he could hear. He asked her to come by, "as soon as possible." Then he looked around the wreck he lived in, turned on some music, and cleaned his crib top to bottom.

When Roselyn walked in, Keith had just finished a second shower. Black Nike shorts, ankle socks, no shirt—he fell into the La-Z-Boy with a damp towel around his neck while she channel-surfed. Minutes passed, quiet stretching, her patience thinning at the weight in his eyes.

"I spent half the night crying because I couldn't bond you out," she said finally. "Me and Poochie ran all day facing one rejection after the next. I'm just happy you're home. When you called today it made my whole day brighter."

Silence again. That trademark glint lived in his eyes whenever he looked at her, but tonight it held something deeper, rawer.

He spoke low but steady. "I could sit here and tell you I love you, but you already know that. Right now my life is all fucked up—and that's on me. Maybe tomorrow, maybe next week, but I'm probably going back in. Baby, can you—wait, let me finish—can you... I don't want to lose you, Rose. My whole foundation gets rebuilt just hearing your voice. When I see your face, this thirsty man gets a full glass of water. Look at me. Really look, and you'll see every inch of my soul."

He swallowed, gathered himself. "Can you see spending the rest of your life with me while I try to make my life mean something to us both?"

"Yes," she cut in, firm. "I can see myself spending my life with you. You got issues—who doesn't? I'm spoiled, selfish sometimes, and concerned as a mother... but I'm comfortable with who I am. I love you, Keith. You're my man. My dude. And no matter where you are or for how long, I'm staying down with you—one hundred and one percent."

The words would've knocked him over if he hadn't already been sitting down. He knew the door back to a cell would swing again; that certainty haunted the love they tried to make afterward. He reached for her with his heart, but the coming distance dimmed the heat around the edges.

Chapter 58

"Keith."

"Huh? I hear you, beautiful. What's up?"

"Oh—I thought you were asleep."

"Nah. Just thinking," he said, fingers combing her hair. "Talk to me."

"Yesterday, after me and Poochie ran all over and I still couldn't get you out, I went home... our song came on, and I cried myself to sleep listening to Anthony Hamilton."

"What's the crazy part?" he asked, rubbing her back now.

"That's when I realized I'm completely in love with you—and there's nothing I can do about it," Roselyn whispered, cheek on his chest.

"So you been in denial—that's what you telling me?"

"Denial? Boy, stop," she laughed. "We both stay so busy surviving, who got time to diagram feelings?"

Keith kissed her hair. The night thinned, morning crept in, and the clock kept moving toward whatever was next.

***

Dear Roselyn,

My Rose,

The time I've spent inside of one prison or another is my biggest regret. I miss your laugh as much as I miss that scratch in your voice when you get passionate. It's been three weeks since I last heard you. I'm wondering: do you remember our love-making to "The Doves of January," as heat, passion, and power had us drifting?

I'm sitting here listening to Anthony Hamilton as I write this line after line—his songs settle me and stir me all at once. Are you receiving some storm of your own? I'm not saying this to keep you; I need to get real for real. Here there's a hard kind of hope.

— Keith B.

***

"BAYLOR! Report to GED!" a C.O. barked through the speaker.

"Damn," Keith muttered to his cellie while tying state boots. "White folks always want a brother to jump running when they call."

"Listen, young blood," the old-school bunkie said, "ain't nothing more important than that paper. Go beat they education down."

Keith had been grinding three months toward this day. Nobody knows what they can do till they try something different. One long afternoon he signed up for GED. Two years later, back in, he'd finally stuck the landing—class time, homework, quiet pride.

"Please be seated, gentlemen," said a slim instructor with a calm voice. "I'll walk you through a small process before we start. My name is Howard Bell. I'm licensed by the State of Georgia to administer this exam. Be proud of yourselves for the work you did to get here. There are eighteen of you today—eighteen out of hundreds—so give yourselves a pat on the back. Relax. Do your best."

Packets slid down rows. Number-2 pencils tapped. Names bubbled. Socials squared. The room settled into a hum of breathing and turning pages.

"The first section will be writing, followed by literature. These two parts will be graded together. Good luck."

It was going to be a long day for this set of convicts—not just a test on paper, but a challenge to their minds and spirits. Keith straightened the booklet, exhaled slow, and began.

Chapter 59

Letter from Roselyn

Hey baby,

I hope you're doing well. I know we haven't talked, and I feel like I need to be honest about some things that been on my mind. First—I miss you terribly. I'm trying to handle it, but it's been hard not having you when I want you, especially when I need you. I said I'd stay down with you through all this, and that's still true. But some nights I go quiet and numb, like your being gone is easier to carry if I don't feel everything at once.

I want you and I'll be here for you, but there are parts of this I have to walk through alone. Since you been locked, I found myself waiting on your call just to breathe better for a few hours. I hate that I can't talk to you when I need to—that's been unbearable. Maybe I'm just frustrated and needed to vent a little. Bear with me while I get my feelings sorted.

I told you I'm staying down—one thing you should already know is I'm true to my word. I don't know where we'll stand after this is over, but love has not been easy on me right now. I need you, but I can't see you or talk to you because you're in prison; then I feel guilty for being mad, because none of this is simple or fair. Please know I miss you so much. I've been doing too much alone—life feels like a version of sorrow, doubt, frustration, anger... and hope.

Stay down. I love you, baby.

— Roselyn

***

"Yo, Key-Man! Chow call," Techwood said in the doorway.

"What's on the menu, lil' buddy?" Keith asked.

"Chili with rice. My maw's favorite."

"No thanks, playboy. I'll pass on that bullshit," Keith laughed, sliding Roselyn's letter back into the envelope and tucking it inside his locker.

"Old chin-chillin' rich ass, huh?" Techwood joked.

"Man, fuck you, Techwood! With your good halitosis ass," Keith shot back, both of them cracking up.

When the door shut, silence came heavy. Keith sat on the bunk, pulled out his CD player, and slid in Anthony Hamilton. "I Know What Love's All About" washed over the cinderblock walls. The words got to him—the way memory can feel like joy and pain at the same time. You can't just go meet the person who used to be your warm place; circumstances keep you from what your soul really wants. And then sometimes somebody new shows up and turns your life around, gives you structure, keeps you off the streets, has you in church on Sundays, saving money, writing your name in a new direction. *I can say I knew love because of you...* The hook kept circling while he stared into the middle distance.

Old School came back from chow, rolled up a cigarette, and watched the younger man's face. He'd seen that look too many times.

"Earth to Keith. Starship to young blood," Old School said, waving his hand.

"What's up, Pop?"

"Lil' buck, I wanna share a dose of *game* with you—if you got time for an old man."

"Always," Keith said.

"This ain't the pep talk. This one can make you or break you," Old School told him. "Not everybody can handle the uncut truth. Those who do, get blessed with a more valuable life."

He locked eyes with Keith. "Twenty years ago I thought I was on top. Six cars, a condo in Buckhead, a house in Tucker, so much money I only counted the big bills. I *was* the man—or so I thought. In the end I got played out of everything, including my freedom. That's part of the game we chose."

"Hold up now, Pop," Keith cut in. "If you about to tell me accept a chick shittin' on me—nah, you trippin'."

"I ain't telling you to accept *that*. I'm telling you to see things for what they *are,* not what they *appear* to be. Let me ask: who sends you money so your black behind can be comfortable right now?"

"My girl—Tameka. Soblack."

"And who mails you packages? Drives down that highway to see you?"

"Soblack," Keith admitted.

"Then riddle me this: why you wasting time trying to love the wrong chick? Because that girl Roselyn—as much as I hate to tell you—she don't care about you the way you care about *her*. If you can't shake the spell, you might as well turn in your player card, player."

The words stung because some part of them rang. Keith said nothing. The Hamilton track kept spinning, and the cell got small.

Chapter 60

It was the first of many hard talks. Old School became a walking foundation—street knowledge plus patient guidance. He'd end up one of the first folks to read Keith's pages when he started writing for real.

Almost six months later, Mail Call delivered a fat stack. Keith flipped through—Soblack, Angel, and finally, tucked underneath, letters from Roselyn. He put on Ne-Yo this time, kicked back, and saved hers for last.

***

Out in the free world, Poochie laced up sneakers while Roselyn tied her curls in a scarf.

"Rose, you wrote Keith?" Poochie asked as they headed out for their walk.

"Not in a few months," Roselyn said. "I plan to tonight."

"You *plan* to? Girl, you better more than plan. He's in there doing time—least you can do is visit," Poochie pressed.

Roselyn flinched. "You don't know everything about me and Mr. Baylor. I ain't getting into it all. But what I'm *not* gonna do is pull up and find that chick Soblack there too."

"What are you supposed to do?" Poochie stopped, hands on hips. "Be a *woman*. That's what. Last I checked, Keith Baylor's in love with *you*. Not that other female. Since when you become a punk, Rose?"

"Fuck you, Poochie! If I'm a punk, then point me to the uniform," Roselyn shot back, storming ahead—then slowing. The anger drained out as quick as it flared. Poochie caught up, cupped Roselyn's face in both hands, and made her meet her eyes.

"You hurt," she said softly. "I know. But at some point you gotta decide—love him or let him go. Life ain't gonna pause."

They walked in silence, then fell back into laughter and trash talk like always. Back at Poochie's apartment, Roselyn hugged her friend and headed home, mind racing. She knew Keith was too much of a man to accept half-love. She was stuck—fear on one side, feeling on the other. In her small, neat office with a mug of hot chocolate, she finally sat down to write.

Letter from Roselyn

Hey babe,

How you doing? Still liking red bottoms? (Kidding—I know you living state-issue now.) I need to say what's real, from the heart.

Last time we talked you said you questioned my feelings because of something I did—maybe something I said. My reply is simple: I speak from the heart. Sometimes it comes out ugly, through anger or hurt, but it still *comes from the same place.*

I haven't heard your voice in a minute. I saw two missed calls but couldn't catch them—work had me locked. Hopefully we'll talk this Sunday on the stranger-sounding phone.

Keith, why do you keep saying you're a failure? I admit, there was a moment I wondered too—*because you were gone,* not because you ain't a man. You are a *good* man. That's why I love you, want you, and plan on keeping you. Our situation is strange, but I'll be okay—and so will we.

Let me share a few memories that are precious to me:

- When we shut down that convo in my Audi, the very last deep talk—we were honest in a way that scared me, and I miss that.
- When you called me from the funeral home at your cousin's wake—I felt honored you wanted me to be the voice you leaned on. It took a lot of heart to dial me then.
- When I walked into the barbershop and your eyes lit up—everybody in there knew I was yours. I *was* gorgeous that day, if I say so myself. Ha!
- At my birthday party—after I blinked the Apple Martinis out my eyes—I saw you and thought, *damn, that's my baby,* stepping on necks.

I could go on, but my hand is cramping. Stay down, baby. Take care of yourself.

PS: I really, really, *really* miss your laugh.

— Roselyn

Chapter 61

Keith finished the last line and scowled. "What the *fuck* is this, Old School? She playing head games?"

"I don't know what's in that woman's mind," Old School said, calm. "What I *do* know—if you let 'em, females will juggle a brother's heart. My read? She misses you and the guilt kicked in. That cousin part is exactly what it is. Advice: read it again. Then again. Give it a day or two before you respond. You can't afford to be off-point with that one."

He leaned forward. "Tell me: you step to her in the beginning—or she come to you?"

"I stepped," Keith said.

"Damn," Old School sighed. "You see, she thinks a little like a dude. You can't treat her like any normal female or it all goes left."

Keith's face betrayed everything—the love, the confusion, the heat. Old School wasn't done.

"Real men are *forged,* not made overnight," he said. "You already got command about you. You ain't in here frontin' for these C.O. bitches. Now focus on Keith Baylor. Not Roselyn. Not nobody else."

"Pop, I don't got time to—"

"You *do,*" Old School cut him off. "Just like she should give you one hundred percent respect, you gotta give one hundred to your own standards. Let me say it plain: Queen behavior belongs in the front row. Bleacher bitches belong outside. A real woman—no matter her color—*honors* her man when she's dealing with a man. In other words: if she wants to be treated like a queen, she better acknowledge her king. If she don't, tell that punk to keep it moving. If she ain't queen material?"

"She got no business in a player's orbit," Keith finished, managing a grin.

They kept building, trading lines of game and lines of reflection. Keith tucked away the pieces that mattered, the ones he could live by—not just write.

***

At The Blazing Saddle, TyRo slipped on heels. "Blackgirl, what time you leaving in the morning?"

"Six-fifteen," Soblack said, checking her bag.

"I was gonna ask for a ride home."

"Passion and Suede riding with me—we heading straight to see Keith. But ask Sultry to drop you; she'll swing you."

TyRo squinted. "Can I ask you something?"

"You can *ask,*" Soblack smirked. "Don't mean I'll answer."

"How you allow your man to see other females?"

"First off—Keith is *my* man. Ain't no gray in that. Second, they going to see him *with me.* And last—he don't do them like that."

"But what if I told you Keith—"

"TyRo," Soblack warned, "a bitch can't tell me shit about my man. Let's kill that convo before you mess up my good mood."

The club was packed to the rafters. At 2:30 a.m., Soblack was in the dressing room sipping water when Passion burst in, breathless.

"Black! Girl, guess who out there making it rain and stuntin'?"

"Who?"

"Babyboy."

Soblack rolled her eyes. "Family?"

"Yeah, and your buddies TyRo and Suede out there scooping every dollar they can for a care package to send Keith," Passion said, pacing. "You should go curse Babyboy out."

"For what? He ain't worth my breath. My man don't need nothing from him anyway. I just hope he gone by the time we clock out so we can make some money," Soblack said, taking another sip.

They showered, paid the house, and hit the expressway just after sunrise—Soblack at the wheel, Passion wide awake clowning, Suede knocked out in the backseat. By the time the prison came into view, three fine women stepping through intake together was all anybody could talk about.

And inside, word would travel fast: Keith Baylor had a line of love waiting in the visiting room.

Chapter 62

"Yo, Key-Man—I saw you puttin' on down in vis-to, baby!" Black Mike from Collier Park hollered across the chow hall.

"No doubt, my guy," Keith grinned, sliding onto the steel bench. Rod and Techwood were already posted up. Trays steamed. Conversation crackled.

"Say it, player," Techwood teased. "Right now? If I had your hand I'd throw mine away."

"And your ass would be handless," Keith shot back.

"Bullshit, Big Dog," Mike laughed. "Strip-club cousins came through to see you, your book 'bout to drop, and you just got your GED. You on a roll."

"That's all true," Rod added. "And I asked the Warden to put you on the mic at graduation."

"Supposed to talk Monday," Keith said. "We'll see what's crackin'."

"When Vic say the book coming?" Mike asked.

"Soblack told me they need a cover for *A+ Hustler* right after the edits, then we good. Next she dropping Part Two—*Crack Ashes*. I'm already working on Part Three and another joint. I'm letting my girl handle the business end."

"Bet. Finish this grub and let's hit the yard," Mike said, standing with Rod.

Keith tried to eat, but everybody in the room kept stopping him to slap hands, to speak life, to ask for pages. Respect felt good; the price was patience. That night he prayed for tolerance, endurance, and humility. He was beginning to see, on a small scale, how much God might have coming his way.

***

“Hey, Meka,” Angel said, opening the back door of Keith’s 300 and lifting a sleepy toddler from the car seat. “Thank you for what you do for me and my baby.”

“Girl, it’s nothing—for real,” Tameka (Soblack) said, reaching to help, settling Shaketa into her own backseat. “You know Keith left a little money to help with you and Keta.”

“Yeah, you told me when Keta was born,” Angel nodded. “But you coulda been like most females and just took the money and said ‘forget me.’”

“Those sisters the ones who messed it up for the real ones,” Soblack said. They hugged.

Sometimes Soblack would meet Angel and take Shaketa for a few days so Angel could study and work extra hours—nursing school didn’t play. The dancers at The Blazing Saddle spoiled the little girl rotten. Even sometimes-stuck-up Sultry popped up with new toys and clothes for Keith’s daughter.

What Soblack didn’t know was that watching how she loved Shaketa was what made Keith fall for her. Time and circumstances moved him forward; piece by piece Roselyn Moore was lifted out of his heart and spirit.

***

Letter from Keith to Roselyn

Hello Roselyn,

Long time, no hear. I’m sure this letter’s a surprise. I hope it finds you well.

I finally got my GED and start trade school in two weeks. My first book, *A+ Hustler,* is slated to be released in three months. I just finished a new story called *Replace Tears with Blood,* and it kicked my muse awake.

Let me say this plain: it's wicked how you ain't even come down to see a brother. Sometimes I'll be listening to the radio and a song you loved slides into my headphones and lights a memory—and I swear I can smell your perfume—but I know that's just my mind joking with me.

As the years go by I've gotten better at handling my feelings about you. I don't even know how I feel about that. I do know this: all I ever asked you to do these past few years was *come see me.* Not just 'cause I miss you, not even 'cause we seriously need to talk, but because I'm in love with you.

I guess I've been forced to realize, respect, and accept a hard truth: it ain't possible for me to love enough for two people. I'm sorry it couldn't turn out better for us. What we want and what we need are two different things.

I'm gonna get out your hair now so I can work on my speech for tomorrow's graduation program. Take care of yourself and be good.

Love always,

Keith

Chapter 63

While Keith wrote that letter, Soblack, TyRo, and three-year-old Shaketa were at Lenox Mall, doing a girls' day—laughing at the little one as much as she laughed at them. By nine, Soblack had Keta home, bathed, and surrendering to sleep.

Keith called at ten.

"Hey, baby girl."

"Hey, baby. Let me step in the other room—Keta just knocked out."

"Damn. I was hoping I could talk to my mini-me."

"Sir, you're gonna have to call *tomorrow*. Your princess ain't a light switch."

"She sleep hard?"

"Like a brick," she smiled. "How you holding up?"

"I'm good. Still working on my writing. Just finished *Replace Tears with Blood*. Feel pretty good in spite of the circumstances, you know?"

"I'm proud of you, Mr. Baylor."

"Proud of me for what, Meka?"

"For doing it the best way you can. You're a man, and you know it."

"Yeah? Well—you know what it is, *Mrs.* Baylor..."

Silence. Then a soft, shocked laugh that almost turned to tears.

"Mr. Baylor... where did *that* come from?"

"It came out true—that's why it slipped out," he said. "Look, I won't waste my phone minutes with a long speech. Just sit with this: how would it be if we were to get married? 'Cause I'd love to have you as my wife."

"You got sixty seconds before it cuts—"

"I know. We'll talk tomorrow. I love you, Blackgirl. See you at the graduation Tuesday, right?"

"Right," she whispered.

She couldn't sleep afterward—happy, dazed, a little off-balance. She knew Keith was about commitment and staying. For once, life felt like the right choice was choosing her back.

Later, Keith caught Q.

"What up, Big Bro? Thought the dead finally decided to call me," Q joked.

"Man, I'm just doing time," Keith said. "But yeah—I asked Tameka about becoming my wife."

"Woooow. So you finally giving Blackgirl her propers."

"She earned that much—and more."

"You need anything?"

"Yeah. Find me a ring. For her. For me."

"Damn, you serious serious," Q laughed. "Say less. I'll scout a few, keep it in budget, and hit you in a couple days with how to play it."

"Bet."

They hung up. Q dialed Poochie. "Well, well, Rose—it look like you out the paint," he said, cracking up. Then he sobered. Grown folks' choices ain't easy; the heart and the head don't always agree. Sometimes all you can do is pray for the wisdom to do right by both.

Chapter 64

"Today we are proud of the men graduating from GED and Trade School," Deputy Warden Chester said into the mic, opening her remarks to the packed gym of staff, convicts, and visitors. "These young men made a choice—to better themselves in a hard situation, under not-so-pleasant circumstances. Lord Jesus, I don't think *I* could've passed that GED thing—let alone do it while locked up."

Laughter rolled around the bleachers.

"I've had the blessing of meeting a very special young man," she continued. "He came in with a whole lot of fire. It was that determination to do something with his life that brought him to our attention—and, oh, how he shocked people here."

"Would you please welcome Hollywood Hall's own... Keith Baylor!"

Black stood and clapped like everyone else as her man strode to the stage. Deputy Chester gave him a small nod and stepped aside.

"Good morning," Keith said.

"Good morning," the gym answered.

"I don't know exactly what I did to shock so many people," he smiled. "So let's give that credit to God. Amen?"

A soft chorus: "Amen."

"To everybody who took a day off work to be here, to every single person in attendance—thank you. Thank you for taking time to support a group of men most of society has written off. From the bottom of my heart, thank you.

"Knowledge unapplied is useless. You can call yourself a man, but just *knowing* you were born male don't count for much. A man must be respectful, reliable, have morals, and take care of the obligations that are his *by default*.

"Not a single one of us in here can honestly say we're 'the man' right now. None of us can pay a bill from in here. None of us can cut the grass, wash the dishes, or take out the trash—small stuff some of y'all weren't doing anyway," he added, drawing a ripple of laughs. "Let me speak on what *needs* speaking on.

"How about being there to read a book to your kids? Being there for your daughters—for the small things, like a walk, or making them laugh. That's gangster. How about if your child got Show and Tell at school—they choose to show *you* off, or tell everyone about you in a way they proud of?

"That, ladies and gentlemen, is the fruit. Not because it's freely passed out, but because real men took the time to be exactly what they were created to be: *men*. Amen."

The crowd stood, clapping. Some smiled, some cried. The rest of the ceremony flowed—diplomas handed to graduates, pictures with family. For a rare moment, men serving time felt treated like human beings.

***

Letter from Roselyn

Keith,

I know you're very surprised to hear from me. I am too. I haven't forgotten you. I always wonder about your wellbeing—your family—and you overall. It's been a while since I communicated, and I take the blame for that, because if nothing else you always made the effort to write me and push me to visit.

I always said I had to make sure *I'm* good first. If I'm not good, how can I make sure anyone else is okay? There's been pressure—life stuff. I had to get me together. Now, I feel like I've lost a lot with you and to be honest, I love you so much. I *do* still love you, Keith, but I just can't love the way I did after being apart so long. I still blame a lot of this on you—and I know that's not gracious—but it is what it is. I just felt the need to say this today, for whatever reason. Only God knows.

Take care, be safe, and stay down, babe.

— Roselyn

Chapter 65

For days after reading Roselyn's letters, Keith simmered—anger, frustration, bitterness—all of it. Feeling neglected by the woman he loved hurt. He turned the pain into fuel, feeding his determination to become a writer. He poured everything into characters on paper. As he finished one story after another, his first readers and loudest supporters were the men walking around him every day. Sometimes he'd pass by and hear two brothers in a heated debate about a character he'd created. The ex–drug dealer with no diploma felt... *lifted.* He'd grab a pen, and a new story would begin.

***

Letter from Keith to Roselyn

Roselyn,

I carefully read the last letter I got from you—what's it been, sixteen, seventeen months since I heard from you? I could tell you how I feel, but I'm sure you already know.

Maybe I should ask what you want from me—but I don't think you know yourself. I'm doing time—something average, everyday people don't do. But on another note, I'm doing other things average, everyday people *don't* do: writing books, getting my GED, now trade school to learn a skill in case the looks take a bad turn.

It was never my dream to come to prison, at any point. Things happen; the answer to "why" ain't always provided. I told you when I was a free man I was a brother from the hood doing the best I could to make it. Back then it didn't matter *how* I made life better, as long as I didn't lay down.

I was born a real motherfucker and I hate disingenuous people. Maybe that's why I dislike the ones quick to preach loyalty, family values, friendship, and respect—without living any of it. Life is a *constant job,* Roselyn. Georgia Power don't stop counting the kilowatts 'cause the day of the week changed. A couple married forty years can wake up tomorrow... and not be married for the day. You get my point.

May God keep you safe and well.

Love,

Keith

***

Year Five

On the outside, a lot had changed—and a lot hadn't. Silk, Muriel, and Q were camped at the barbershop window waiting on Soblack to bring the first box of *A+ Hustler*. Q's phone rang; he didn't need to check the screen.

"Hey, sexy—what's the business?" he answered.

"Boy, I ain't your mama. You so stupid," Stacey (Poochie) laughed. "You still waiting on that book?"

"Yep. Should be here any minute."

"Okay—just left Annette's. Don't forget my copy."

Q's attention snapped back to the glass. Soblack had just pulled up—with Sultry and Suede sliding out behind her. Heads turned—from the chair to the curb, every male eye tracking. Even folks who thought Keith was a ghost could feel it: the hustler-turned-author still moved the street.

Soblack was 100% behind her man, and when he told her his vision, she decided she was gonna *represent*. A few of the girls from the clubs had chipped in to buy a hundred copies, and within an hour twenty-six different dancers had invaded the block.

At 7:30 the phone rang inside the shop.

"What's happening, my player friend?" Silk said.

"Boy, I'm watching this unfold. Tell me this ain't some type of TV pilot," Q laughed.

"Good, Silky. This what I'm talking about. Everything ready?"

"Yep, Key-Man. Me and Q got you covered."

"Well, my man, it's your show. I'll hit you back in thirty."

"Check that," Silk said, and immediately dialed Chef.

"Hey, say, Chef—shine me."

"Okay, my friend. I'm rolling."

Every week Chef parked a little RV in the gas-station lot, two big speakers bolted to the side, blasting the hottest music for the block. Suddenly the music cut. Instant quiet rippled through the crowd as everybody turned toward the trailer.

The most talked-about street book signing in the city was about to jump.

Chapter 66

Every now and then something happens that leaves a permanent print on a person. The memory—good or bad—hangs around for years, and the lucky ones get a handful of moments to look back on with joy, ache, passion, fear, excitement, and love. That's the real honor of genuine companionship: knowing you lived a life that meant something.

Chef stepped out of his trailer carrying a fresh chocolate cake with one fat candle burning dead-center. Q tested the mic, gave it a couple taps, and the crowd in the gas-station lot turned his way.

"Hey—hey—everybody, let me have your attention for a minute," he said. "First off, my man wanted me to tell all of y'all thank you for coming out—in his absence. Even though he ain't here physically, this is still *his* block, *his* show!"

The crowd hollered.

"Aight, enough of the soft stuff—'cause we got some for-real business!" Laughter and ayes rolled back.

Q motioned. "Soblack—my man wanted to show you that 'spending the rest of my life with you' is *exactly* what he means. Come on up here, long-legs, 'cause this candle is for you to blow out for my player partner."

The clapping rose again. Tameka walked up pretty and nervous, trying to hold it in, but that last line had her grinning.

Q leaned to her ear. "Blackgirl, Keith said everything he's becoming is 'cause you never gave up on him. This is for being the special woman you are." He slipped a ring from his left pocket and onto her left ring finger.

"Congratulations, Blackgirl. Thank you for loving that crazy nigga," Q laughed. "I'd kiss you, but you know I like lips."

Tears slid down Tameka's face. Q guided her to the cake to blow out the candle. Piped across the top, in bold white letters, it read *A + Hustler*. Then the music came right back—Bey, Ne-Yo, Rihanna—Chef shook the RV like a club. The strippers danced, the block cheered, silk cut Soblack a big slice, and the rest of the night rolled sweet and loud.

***

Letter from Roselyn

Keith,

I received your last letter the other day and it seems now that you're needing to call me in your salutations. I do have to say I'm much more comfortable with the mailbox addressed and consistent to *me*. Not saying you were disrespectful, but you didn't know. It's my responsibility to inform you.

With that being said, please don't write and send letters here anymore in my name.

I hope you have success in what you're trying to achieve.

— Roselyn

***

Later that day Roselyn stepped out of Stacey's bathroom—company in the house—so she'd used the hall one. Back in Stacey's bedroom, she spotted a thick black paperback on the bed: *A + Hustler*. Her heart kicked. She sat, picked it up, and got lost in the first chapter—didn't even notice Stacey leaning in the doorway smiling.

"Closure your lane done?" Stacey asked, teasing.

Roselyn wiped at her eyes. “Pretty much,” she said with a sad smile. “And to think I just wrote him last week telling him not to write me no more. Poochie, I messed up—for real.”

“The worst part,” she sighed, “is I sent Keith a letter saying don’t contact me no more... because I let Darnell back in.”

“Rose,” Poochie said, soft but firm, “you can’t fix something that broke that far.”

“Keith been gone almost five years,” Roselyn snapped back. “Nobody can expect me to love him the same after being apart so long.”

“Yes they can—if the love you had was real. Your *heart* called you to do something else, and you ignored it.”

“That’s easy for you to say,” Roselyn muttered. “What you do when you lonely and hurting?”

“I pray harder. And I love harder,” Stacey said. “Get over your pride and pray. Tough times come to tough people.”

“Yeah,” Roselyn whispered, hugging her best friend. “Only the strong make it to the end.”

What neither woman knew was that Roselyn’s last letter had done damage beyond repair. The rules of the game had changed, and only a fool plays a game without learning the rules. In Roselyn’s case, it came down to what one woman *wouldn’t* do... and what another one *did*.

Chapter 67

Angel packed Shaketa's bag so her daughter would be ready when Sultry and TyRo came to pick her up for Tameka. It was a little after six. Mother and aunt were having a cordial moment when Renee poked her head in the den.

"Oh—those nasty friends of yours just drove up," Renee sneered.

"Renee, I can halfway understand you being bitter with me," Angel said calmly, "but there's no cause to clown people you don't even know."

"What's to know? They shake their butts for a living."

"And you lay on your back for one," Sultry said, stepping in behind her, TyRo and Angel's sister right behind.

Renee was caught off guard but smoothed her face into a thin smile. "Bitch, please. I hustle for mine. You trickin' wouldn't know nothing about—"

"Oh no she didn't," TyRo barked, pushing past Dee-Dee toward Renee.

Little Shaketa peeked from behind her mama's leg at the bedroom doorway. Seeing Keith's daughter snatched the steam out of Sultry's fuse. She grabbed TyRo's arm and pulled her back.

"Renee, we came with good intentions, 'cause Blackgirl out of town seeing Keith," Sultry warned. "But I promise you—your ass is mine the first chance I get."

"Do it then," Renee snapped. "Ain't nothing between us but air and opportunity."

“Renee, stop acting stupid in front of my niece,” Dee-Dee hissed.

“For what? It ain’t like she don’t hear and see way worse around *they* asses,” Renee shot back.

“That’s foul and you know it,” TyRo said. “Tameka would never do nothing foul around that baby. I’m telling her what you said.”

“Come on, Keta,” Sultry sighed. “Angel, get her bag—we waiting outside.”

The only reason it stayed a standoff was the four-year-old in the house. An hour later, children worked their regular magic, making the bad mind vanish. At TyRo’s apartment, Keta giggled over a video game while Sultry’s phone rang.

“What’s up, girl,” she answered.

“Not much, I’m on the expressway,” Soblack said. “How’s Keta?”

“Good—playing with me and Ty. You home or Ty’s?”

“Ty’s for a minute.”

“Okay, stop by to pick her up. And, Blackgirl—got something to tell you when you get here.”

“Let that mess lie,” TyRo warned after they hung up, bouncing Keta on her lap.

“Hell no,” Sultry said. “You know I’m telling Meka.”

“Blackgirl gonna snap when she hears that garbage. Let it go.”

“Listen—Renee had you ready to jump too, and I bet this ain’t the first time she said something ugly.”

"Who said something ugly?" Suede asked, walking in with Passion.

"Damn," TyRo mumbled. Sultry told it all.

By the time Soblack got to TyRo's, tempers were lit. Suede didn't waste a breath—she and Passion were already lacing shoes. Tameka's face tightened the second she heard it. Ten minutes later TyRo was beeping the horn; Soblack, Passion, Suede, and Sultry were on their way to find Renee.

Renee was at the usual gas station on Jonesboro Road roasting Kathy, the dope fiend who always came up short.

"If you want a twenty, you got eighteen. If you need a fifty, you got forty-five," Renee barked. "I bet your dumb ass do that at KFC too. Stop coming up to me like I'm the motherf—in' Credit Association! I might as well start running two-for-one specials."

Kathy bobbed and grinned through the cussing. The barbershop and the lot were full of men watching the circus. Renee never saw trouble sliding her way—Soblack always kept it clinical.

"I can see you like hearing your own mouth so much you still talking," Tameka said, stepping up. "You got something you wanna say to me?"

"Bitch—please," Renee smirked. "If I feel like saying something to *you,* I'll say it."

Pow. Soblack put a tight right hand on Renee's nose. Stunned a second, Renee launched a hard kick into Tameka's left thigh, knocking her off balance.

It cracked off from there. Two more sisters on the block made the mistake of cheering for Renee.

"That's right, girl—F her up—"

Pow. Sultry stole one of them in the mouth. Passion snatched the other by her hair. Renee hit the ground and the fight turned ugly—for her. Suede and Soblack started kicking and stomping.

Silk saw men rushing out of the barbershop and pushed between bodies—last thing he needed was calling Keith to say his woman caught a case. In seconds the four women were yanked apart and gone. The story ran through the block like lightning; folks would be talking for a while.

Silk slipped back in the shop, pulled out his phone, and called Q.

Chapter 68

"Inmate Keith Baylor. Inmate Keith Baylor—report to Counselor Holmes' office," the speaker droned.

Keith was mid-game in the sink area—no speaker there—so he missed it. Old School heard and poked his head out.

"Yo, young buck—your bull-shit counselor calling you for something."

"Hold my spot, Techwood—I'll be back in a minute."

"Do *you* then, player. Maybe the sorry motherf— finally calling you for something *right* off them speakers."

"Yeah, right. Hell will freeze before they hand a brother good news." Keith grinned anyway and walked.

Eight months had passed since the Renee/Soblack scuffle. Keith, now past five years in, had long lost faith in the system—same as most. Too many men chewed up and spit out. A system that cared less about a man's accomplishments than his number.

"Come on in, Mr. Baylor. Have a seat," Counselor Holmes said, grabbing a stack of forms. "Mr. Baylor, I received a fax to complete a parole summary on you. That means the Board is considering releasing you at some point. I cannot say when. I'll need two different addresses you can parole to, along with those persons' names and phone numbers. If you need to run back to your dorm to get it, I can wait."

***

Three months later, Keith sat on his bunk closing out the last chapter of another story when Old School came in from the kitchen job, sat on the lower bunk, and lit a cigarette.

“Kid, let me rap with you a minute before your homeboys flood in later,” he said.

“What’s up, Pops? Need something done on the street? Say the word.”

“Nah. You already done more than enough putting them canteen bags in my locker. And you like that hustle out the kitchen—you’ll be fine.”

He paused.

“What you plan to do once you walk out tomorrow?”

“Chill for a minute. Then books—and my baby girl. Try to catch up.”

“No doubt. Roselyn know you coming home?”

“Hell *no,* Pops. Ain’t heard from that chick since last summer,” Keith snapped.

The old man’s worry had always been that his roommate would get out and break weak for a woman who left him for dead. He looked into the younger man’s eyes and felt better.

“I know you got a surprise up your sleeve for these knuckleheads tomorrow,” Old School smirked. “Do your thing. Just carry one more thing with you:

“Pick the people around you with care, Keith. Folks out there like vampires—they’ll eat you dry and leave you cold. A old motherf— like me can hope good things for you, but my feelings ain’t worth spit if you don’t chase ’em yourself. I watched you grow as a man. If I helped any, I can go to sleep smiling. Just don’t neglect nothing I told you. Love that young lady like you supposed to—and take care of yourself.”

"Pops, you sure you don't want me to talk to a lawyer or something for you?"

"Boy, you ain't learned yet? The black folks at the Board don't want nothing to do with letting our chocolate asses out, and the black folks *in* here ain't far from being inmates themselves. A sex offender can make parole faster than a brother hustling a few dollars. Get your ass out of here and live. Handle your business. And F anybody feelings who dislike you moving on."

He stood. "Now I'm going to smoke before I remember my 183s gon' be dead before your release hits."

As soon as Old School left, Keith stood, grabbed a pen and a sheet of paper, and copied the old man's info off his state jacket—addresses and all. Real brothers do real things; that's why they're born, not made. The hazel-eyed hustler figured it was his duty to drop money orders on the old man from time to time.

Chapter 69

Tuesday morning, July 10th. Keith was packing property when the line of homies slid through to say goodbye. After the handshakes and hugs, only Techwood lingered.

"Well, Key-Man, the ride in this bull is finally over," Tech said.

"Pretty much a done deal," Keith grinned. "I'ma miss kicking your ass in chess."

"Last I remember I was up one game."

"Line it up on the street, my nigga," Keith laughed.

"No doubt," Tech answered, then got serious. "Look—I got three more years. I ain't asking for pity, but if you could do something nice for my moms..."

"Say less."

When Keith stepped into the hallway with his property, the tier erupted—fifty brothers clapping and yelling.

"Y'all just *seen* a ghost come through this bitch," Keith hollered. "So make sure y'all look out the damn window!"

A half hour later the whole compound shook. A solid-gold Ford Excursion rolled onto the property like a parade float. Every convict ran to a window.

As the truck parked, the last gate buzzed. Keith "Hard-Knock Hustler" Baylor walked out into the sunlight. Soblack, little Shaketa, Angel, Suede, Passion, Sultry, and TyRo piled out. The second Keta saw her daddy she launched herself into his arms. Tameka reached back into the truck and came out with a small Crown Royal bag.

Keith was crisp: all-white suede Sean John warm-up, all-white Timbs. As he walked toward the ride, carrying his daughter, the hood of the Excursion flashed another surprise—serious platinum chain with praying hands for a charm. Hugs, kisses, laughter everywhere. Then everybody slid back in and the hard-knock hustler eased their new ship off the property, cracked the volume, and unleashed thunder.

He knew every eye in the windows was glued to him, so he braked, climbed up on the hood, and gave the yard a salute before sliding back down and peeling away.

Old School stayed in the window long after the parking lot cleared. Techwood returned fifteen minutes later and laid a hand on his shoulder.

"He'll be alright, Pops. Don't worry."

"I know, Woody," the old man said. "He damn sure gave these petty motherf— something to talk about."

"That he did. Hope the streets ready—'cause a real hog coming through."

Old School didn't comment—he agreed. What he couldn't say out loud was he felt for Keith like a father for a son. He was scared he hadn't taught him everything he'd need.

"Pops, what you thinking about?" Tech asked.

"Trying to think up a name for that noise that boy was playing for y'all knuckleheads."

"That was Plies, *'Bust It Baby.'* Come on, Old School. Let's grab some coffee while I enlighten you."

"I'll enlighten *you*, you little shit," the old man laughed, heading for the dayroom.

Keith had exactly twenty-four hours to report to his parole officer, so he wanted to handle a little business first. He dropped everybody at Sultry's new house. Soblack took him to see his attorney/agent. Shaketa slept in her father's arms, refusing to be left—didn't move once as they walked into Rebecca Randle's office.

The beautiful fifty-one-year-old lawyer was on the phone when they came in—and her first thought was *Lord!*

"Give me a chance to look up the information, Dana—I'll call you back, okay?" Rebecca said into the line.

"Has that new guy shown up yet?"

"Yes," Rebecca said, eyes on Keith.

"Is he fine?" Dana asked.

"You wouldn't believe me if I told you. Bye."

She hung up. "Hello, Keith. We finally get to meet away from confinement," she smiled, stepping around the desk to shake his hand.

"Feels good to be free," he said.

"I can understand that, even if I've never been in your situation. Tameka, how are you, girlfriend?"

"Fine, Ms. Rebecca."

"Good. Then take a seat. No sense in all three of us standing—your daughter already found the best spot in the house."

"That's alright," Soblack said. "We just came by to invite you to the barbecue—'cause Mister Knucklehead couldn't wait to see you in person."

"Well thank you, Keith. I'm glad to see you in person too."

"That's good to hear," he grinned. "'Cause we got a whole lot of work to do before our wedding—but we'll talk real soon."

Rebecca Randle—lawyer and now agent—looked forward to talking in depth with her young client. She had a strong feeling that working with Keith Baylor was going to be different... and interesting. What neither of them knew yet was just how hard the hazel-eyed hustler was about to push to make his books bestsellers.

Here are cleaned, continuous versions of Chapters 70–71, the Fans' Message, and the Final Thought. I fixed the OCR noise and kept the voice, slang, and plot intact.

Chapter 70

The cookout for Keith wasn't packed like a block party—he'd told Tameka he didn't want a big crowd. Soblack wanted her man comfortable, period. Angel had already made peace with the fact that nothing was coming between Keith and Tameka. She stood with Tameka, watching Keith chase their daughter through the yard while Rebecca Randle chatted nearby.

"Angel, I ain't so selfish I'm worried about you talking to Keith," Tameka said. "You not gon' offend me. We good. For Keta's sake—go talk to her father."

Angel nodded, nervous, and Tameka gave her a playful push toward the house. Angel caught Keith coming out of the bathroom. For a second it was awkward, then Keith broke the ice.

"You look good, Angel."

"Thanks—and so does our daughter."

"She ever get tired?" Keith grinned.

"Never. She stay on ten. But I think it's 'cause she finally feels home," Angel said, smiling.

"You've done a good job with her."

"I appreciate that, but without my sister and Tameka, it would've been rough."

"I hear you," he said. "Just know—I'm here for you and Keta now. You don't have to worry."

"I know, Keith. Just... get *you* straight first." Angel slipped a small white envelope into his palm. "Pictures. My new number. Her schedule." He hugged her, slid it in his pocket, and exhaled.

Around eight, Silk and Q came through to salute their partner. Silk put five hundred cash in Keith's hand; Nique added an all-black Falcons jacket, an outfit, and another three hundred—"Welcome home, Key-Man." At 9:30, Tameka drove Keith to their *new* house for the first time. Three bedrooms, tastefully furnished—exactly the kind of calm he'd been picturing on long nights.

They made love like people who'd waited too long: bold, tender, intense, exhausted, relieved. Soblack fell asleep on his chest. Thoughts of plans, angles, and better ways to win stacked up in Keith's mind until sleep finally caught him too. Tomorrow would be a new day—and he was going to meet it thinking *strategy*.

***

Across town, Roselyn was getting dressed to go out with Annette and Stacey when Darnell started.

"I *know* you been with that nigga," he snapped.

"F— you, Darnell. I don't know what you talking about," Roselyn said, sliding on earrings.

"I'm talking about how every weekend you and your girls out. Personally, I find that suspect."

"If you wanna go, *come on*. But stop trippin'—you sound stupid."

"Oh, now I'm stupid?" He leaned over the recliner's back. "Bitch, don't get knocked the f— out."

Before he could puff another breath, Annette and Poochie walked in.

"Put your motherf—ing hands on my sister and you won't have hands, buster," Poochie said, dropping her little purse on the table.

"Hey, baby girl, calm down. I was just talking," Darnell smirked. Neither Annette nor Stacey liked him; they tolerated him because Roselyn did.

"You know a lotta men who *talk* about hitting women got control problems," Annette said.

"And too many that threaten it end up doing it," Poochie added.

"Man, get outta here with that Dr. Phil crap," Darnell muttered, standing up and stalking out the room. He was one of those good-looking, good-for-nothing types sisters get snared by because the sex is great. *After* the sex? Nobody asks *then what*.

Roselyn didn't even know where they were headed—it was Annette's turn to pick. Friday traffic glowed around them.

"I'm telling you, Rose," Annette said from the back seat, "it's a matter of time before that negro puts his hands where they don't belong."

"And *that* will be the day I end up in somebody jail for killing a motherf—," Roselyn said from the passenger seat.

"Where we going, girl?"

"A new club—*The Final Live*."

"Oh, I heard about that," Poochie said. "Cool."

"Marv got us VIP passes through his boy," Annette grinned. "But tonight we buying *our* drinks."

"Whatever, girlfriend—not this heifer," Poochie laughed, nudging Roselyn.

A quick quiet washed Roselyn's face. "You mind sharing that sinking thought with us?" Poochie asked.

"Huh? What thought?"

"That hush that got you all quiet."

"It's nothing serious. I'm cool... It's just—Keith been out now for six months and not once has he reached out to anybody *we* know."

Poochie had asked Nique on the low a few times. He never spoke on Keith's business. It was like their relationship and Keith's household were top secret—which, truth was, Nique knew told him everything he needed to.

Chapter 71

"Okay, Keith—we've got the new release set up," Rebecca said. The four of them—Tameka, Keith, Dana, and Rebecca—sat around a table at the Starbucks in Ansley Park, Monday at noon. Keith had been home a year. *A + Hustler* had moved almost 45,000 copies and was still selling. He'd driven all over the state promoting—tired but locked in. Old School was still his mentor, and Keith kept the old man's canteen account heavy and his mama taken to dinner once a month.

"So," Rebecca continued, "you *don't* want to do a part two launch in a bookstore like most authors. Care to enlighten us?"

Keith smiled. "Saturday night. Big release party at Club *Final Line*. I'm giving away my 300 Chrysler to one lucky person who buys the right book."

"What?!" Rebecca yelped. "We don't have that many books, and that beautiful car is *paid for*."

"I know. So is my Excursion," Keith said. "It's just a car, Rebecca—calm down."

"Baby—she's right. We don't even have two thousand on hand," Soblack said.

Keith still smiled. Dana had kept his plan quiet like he'd asked. "Time for final arrangements. I need both of y'all."

"Dana, you talk to Vicki?"

"Yes. She got the check Friday—books ship tomorrow. I'm also paying all the major Atlanta stations today, like you wanted—"

"Dammit, Keith," Rebecca cut in, "if you're paying for this out of pocket, you'll be flat broke before Friday."

"Yep," he said. "But I'll have made five times that by Monday morning."

"Blackgirl, I'm gonna need the ladies' help again," he told his wife.

"A'ight, baby. You sure?"

"Absolutely."

Tameka wasn't about to steer her man off what his heart was set on. If he was pushing, she was pushing—right beside him. Rebecca shook her head, then caught herself smiling. If everybody was this determined to go for broke on *Shades of a Gangster,* then hell—she'd lace up too.

***

"Girl, look at this crowd," Annette said from the driver's seat. "Keith's new book must be the truth."

"I feel like a teenage girl on her first date," Roselyn said, nerves jumping.

"Then don't sit here looking crazy—go *get your man,*" Poochie said, grinning.

It was Annette and Poochie's idea to pull up at the signing at **This Coffee House** on Roswell Road. Nobody expected a line down the block on a Saturday night. Keith had been on his feet for hours, only sitting long enough to sign, sell, and tell folks about the club event.

Roselyn walked in alone, listening to the chatter, trying to build up nerve. Keith was busy, head down, signing... then he looked up for the next buyer and locked eyes with *her*. It thumped him in the gut—the sexy, beautiful Roselyn smiling right in his face. Time took a breath. Neither of them said a word for several seconds.

Soblack, clock always in mind, leaned in Keith's right ear and broke the spell. "Sweetheart, we need to roll. You've got another signing *and* a 9:15 interview. Dana's already outside starting up the car."

"Yeah... okay, baby," Keith said, standing.

"Hello, Roselyn. Want me to sign that real quick for you?"

"Yes, Keith. Thank you. Can you put: 'To Roselyn, my special friend'?"

He paused, then wrote instead:

> *"Everyone's perception is different—and sometimes illusions get confused with reality."*
>
> — Keith Baylor

"Roselyn Moore," he said, handing the book back, "this is my wife, Tameka Baylor. Tameka—Roselyn." He kissed his little lady to the crowd, shook Tray's hand, then turned and moved with his team—leaving a very still Roselyn behind.

When Roselyn came out, Poochie and Annette were leaning on the car watching Keith pull off with the two other women.

"Girl, did you get his number? What happened?" Annette asked, lit up.

"No, hun—I didn't." Roselyn passed the book to Poochie. Poochie opened to the inside cover and blinked.

"Damn... f—."

"What that mean?" Annette asked, confused.

"It mean I messed up," Roselyn said, sliding into the passenger seat. "I really messed up."

A Message to My Fans (from Gymaco)

Everyone who's read my work—your thoughts, opinions, and support have been priceless.

To Rod, Tray, JB, MacArthur, Eric, and my man Kevin Moore—you've ridden every sentence as I put pen to paper, sharing the feelings I poured into every line. Thanks, fellas, for being on the winning team.

One more bestseller is out the way and I'm moving on to the next, so get ready for me to drive y'all crazy all over again. To all my present and future readers: I'm forever humble in this—God gave me a talent I didn't even know was inside me. Please know I'll keep praying and working hard to make each story capture my fans, and I hope never to be a disappointment in respect to my craft.

Much love,

Gymaco

Final Thought

Never at any point did I plan to write a book like this. When I first put pen to paper, I had no idea where I was going. Truth and the thoughts I was battling carried me the rest of the way. I used a few brothers as composites and built this story. I wanted to hit the many things that happen in a certain kind of relationship. Even though this is fiction, I wrote from a real-life perspective.

In my own relationships I was forced to learn some hard lessons, and I pulled from those trials to shape this tale. No one—*no one*—is exempt from making bad decisions or from the joys and pains of being in love. Remember: great sex, good times, and good company are easy to find—but they can be illusions. At the end of the night, when you're alone, you can feel hollow and empty.

Real love can't be played with. It takes *two* people. God knows I've made my share of mistakes, but if I've learned anything, it's this: when completeness shows up—with respect, trust, support, communication, and understanding—you know the love for your other half is real. No amount of money equals it in value, because what you have is *priceless*.

I wanted the underdogs to come out on top this time—and I wanted to share real pain too. Hopefully I've been blessed to do both—and more. From the very bottom of my heart, thank you for reading my work.

Stay blessed, and stay tuned for what's next.

— Gymaco

www.ingramcontent.com/pod-product-compliance
Lightning Source LLC
Chambersburg PA
CBHW060359310726
48976CB00003B/874

* 9 7 9 8 8 9 8 6 4 0 1 0 1 *